Pups and Poison

A Vampire Veterinary Mystery

Book 2

Sedona Jade

With Amy Stake & Sedona Ashe

Cover and interior artwork by Cauldron Press

www.cauldronpress.ca

A huge thank you to-

Allison Woerner for Alpha Reading.

Maxine Meyer for Copy Editing.

Emily Levault for Proofreading & Editing.

PUPS
AND
POISON

A VAMPIRE VETERINARY MYSTERY

SEDONA JADE
WITH AMY STAKE

CONTENTS

CHAPTER ONE

A werewolf, a mermaid, and a pixie walk into a bar... If you're thinking that's the start of a bad joke, you'd be correct. Except the joke, in this case, would be my life. I stared at the three supernaturals in front of me and frowned.

Being a vet in a town as odd as Bluejay Falls was hard enough; add in being a vampire running a veterinary clinic to help magical creatures and you'd get an idea of the types of challenges I faced on a daily basis. To make matters worse, I was currently down a vet tech, which was how I ended up conducting what had quickly become the interview from Hades.

I continued to study the two contenders and the corner of my lips down-turned further. The mermaid was completely untrained, and while she'd be great at putting people at ease, as her species tended to do, I couldn't afford her mixing up medications or breaking expensive equipment. Not to mention that she refused to tie up her knee-length hair, which would definitely get her into trouble sooner or later with an unruly patient. I barely hid my cringe as she flipped her mane of golden locks over her shoulder, accidentally slapping Bree, my pixie vet tech, in the face.

My eyes slid to the second candidate who sat next to her on the plastic chairs of the waiting room. He was easily the tallest man I'd ever seen. His height wasn't exactly a surprise, since werewolves on average tend to be taller than most humans and paranormals, but he had taken it to a whole different level—literally. If he'd been any taller, his head would have bumped against the ceiling. The young man scowled, his eyes narrowing on the competition sitting next to him.

Don't worry, kid, I thought. *Neither of you is a good fit for the job.*

But just because I knew what had to be done, didn't mean it was easy. This was the worst part of running your own business. Forcing a smile, I tilted my head, letting Bree know I wanted her to join me in the back office so we could come up with the best way to let these two down easy.

As I walked, the sound of the pixie's glittery boots clicking on the tile floor echoed down the long white hallway as she hurried after me. Ever since she'd colored her hair to match the rainbow of her pixie soul—her words, not mine—she seemed to have an extra pep in her step.

Though maybe she was just excited at the possibility of finally getting some help around the veterinary clinic.

While Bree and I had been able to handle the work ourselves in the past, recently, the clinic had been the busiest since I'd opened it. We were overflowing with regular and supernatural patients, and after the tragic loss of my previous tech, it was high time for someone else to step in and help. I wasn't so much of a control freak that I couldn't admit I needed help. Shocker for a vamp, I know.

Sunny Days Veterinary Clinic was growing in leaps and bounds and we simply couldn't keep up on our own.

Turning the stainless-steel handle, I stepped into the break room and scanned the space carefully. When I found what I was looking for, a smile tugged at my lips.

"Byrd is here." I pointed to the top shelf of a tall book-case and the tiny black bat curled up in a ball in the corner.

"Finally," Bree huffed, pretending to be annoyed. "I've been looking for the little bugger all evening. We need to put a bell on him or something."

Chuckling, I reached up to stroke the silky black fur between his ears. In response, Byrd purred, then tucked his nose under his wing and returned to his nap. I'd rescued him some time back. Once he'd fully healed, I'd tried to release him, but the sly little bat kept finding his way back inside the clinic. I'd begun to enjoy the daily game of hide-and-seek with the adorable bat and had finally given up trying to shoo him back outside. Now he spent most of his time between the clinic, hitching a ride to my house inside my purse, and occasionally going for a sleepover with Bree.

It was nice having him around, despite the mess he usually left behind.

And my parents said I'd die a loner…

Checking the clock on the wall, I grimaced. It was almost eight in the evening, so we only had an hour before we had to open the clinic doors. Being the only clinic in town that operated from dusk till dawn meant that our hours were wonky, but surprisingly, it was actually great for business. We provided emergency care for regular animals through the front door, and always kept the back door unlocked for the supernatural to creep through in the dead of night without being detected.

It was a win-win for all. Plus, it gave me a chance to stay true to my vamp self.

I was a natural born vampire, so with enough sunscreen, I could tolerate the sun. But I tried to stay consistent with my species branding and everyone knows that nighttime and vampirism go together like salsa and tortilla chips.

"So," I said, leaning my hip against the exam table that now served as our breakroom table, "what do you think?"

Bree's nose twitched and her brow creased. "Please tell me you have other interviews lined up."

"That was the last of them," I sighed. "I know what you mean, though. Neither of them is a good fit, but we're running out of supernaturals who have experience in the field. It's easier to find a human tech, but convincing them to work odd hours while also hiding our little secret from them makes it beyond difficult to keep them. I really wanted to hire a supernatural this time and make our lives a little easier."

"We'll find someone. Don't give up." Bree flashed me her pearly whites and brushed past me, heading for the small fridge in the corner of the room.

She opened the door, then used a key from her chain to open the small hidden drawer in the back. With a creak, the hidden portion of the fridge slid open to reveal an array of blood juice boxes.

Snatching up a Crimson Quench, she tossed it at me. "Eat," she commanded. "You look like the walking dead. And not the cool, brain-eating kind."

Grimacing, I meekly shoved the plastic straw into the box and downed the carton in one long sip. My mood instantly refreshed.

It was miraculous the things today's science could do for a vamp; all the benefits of human blood produced in a lab and packaged in a cute, discreet container. Don't worry kids, no humans had been harmed for this vamp's digestion. It was shocking there were still vampires out there who hadn't converted to the good fake stuff. Fools and charlatans, as my mom called them. Well, she used more choice words, but that woman could swear like a sailor in a pirate movie.

Grabbing a napkin, I dabbed the corner of my mouth. "I'm starting to lose hope we'll ever find someone."

"Have you considered you might need to branch out?"

"Hiring a human again?" I lifted an eyebrow. "No, thank you. After what happened with Justin, I can't risk it.

Humans are too... sensitive. And we need someone who understands the clients. *All* of them."

The pixie opened her mouth to reply but her words were cut off by a gut-wrenching scream emanating from the waiting area.

Moving swiftly, I tossed the blood box in the trash, checked on Byrd—still fast asleep—and ran after Bree down the corridor. We darted past examination rooms and the charts hanging on the wall at the speed of, well, supernatural beings.

My feet skidded to a stop as we reached the waiting area and my jaw hit the floor. "What in the smithereens is going on here?"

Every chair in the room was turned upside down and several of the pictures we'd carefully hung on the walls to welcome patients lay crumpled on the tile floor. A strange salt and sulfur smell filled the room, slightly reminiscent of boiled eggs and the Atlantic Ocean.

The werewolf had embedded his long, razor-sharp claws into the ceiling and was hanging there, mid-shift. His matted tail swung from side to side as he tried to stay as far off the ground as possible. Beneath him, the mermaid seethed with rage and snatched at his tail with her manicured nails.

"Can someone please explain to us what happened?" I ground out through gritted teeth.

The wolf's glowing eyes flicked to my face. "Ask her!" he grunted. "The insane fish attacked me!"

At that, the mermaid hissed and jumped higher. Her

nails made contact with his tail and she yanked, tearing off a mat of fur in the process. The wolf shrieked, releasing the same high-pitched wail we'd heard earlier.

My gaze met Bree's, and I tried to remain calm while watching her stifle a laugh.

"Not helping," I said out of the side of my mouth.

She chuckled. "All right, fine. Give me a minute."

Wiggling her shoulders as though shaking off any stress, the pixie closed her eyes, and I watched in awe as she released her magic. Her hair swarmed her face as sparkles swirled around her like a colorful tornado that moved so fast, I swore it lifted her off the ground a few inches. Opening her eyes, she gave me a cheeky grin before stretching out her hands and sending her magic surging toward the bickering pair.

The mood in the waiting room changed instantly. A sense of calm filled my chest, and my shoulders slumped in relief. Before me, the mermaid froze, her eyes widening. The werewolf let go of our butchered ceiling tiles and lowered himself back down, blinking in confusion. Bree's magic had affected all of us.

I smiled. Yep, pixies were freaking amazing.

"Now," I said again, eyeing the befuddled pair in front of me. "Someone explain."

Spell broken, the two began to talk over each other until I couldn't understand a word either one was saying.

Raising my hand to shut them up, I ordered, "One at a time, please. You go first," I told the werewolf.

"I was just trying to be nice, and she lost it," he muttered, side-eyeing the mermaid.

Her sharp teeth flashed. "You asked me if I sleep in a tank."

"It's a valid question," the wolf remarked with a shrug. "I've never met a fish-girl before."

The mermaid's violet eyes flared, and she looked at me as if to say, *"Do you see what I have to deal with?"*

I cringed and fixed the young man with a serious glare. "You do understand how that's insulting, right? Paranormals need to learn to be more respectful of other species. It's bad enough that we are portrayed as monsters in human media. We don't need to be attacked and hurt by other supernatural beings as well."

His gaze fell and his tail drooped onto the floor. "You're right. Sorry."

"Next time, think twice before you speak once." Shaking my head, I turned in a slow circle, taking in the destroyed waiting room. "Never mind. You two are going to help us clean this place up before we open the doors for the night. Now."

Bree appeared, shoving a broom into the mermaid's arms, while I led the werewolf to the other side of the room to begin righting the chairs. We did our best to keep them far away from each other, not quite trusting the tenuous truce to hold.

As we worked to clean the mess they'd created, my chest tightened. It was nearly time to open, and I wasn't sure we could finish in time. The last thing I needed was for word to get out that I ran a shifty operation at the clinic. Bluejay Falls was great, but it had all the markings of a small town… and that included all the gossip.

One word about the state of this place and people would be talking about us for weeks… or at least until the next scandal or mystery arose. I couldn't afford any extra scrutiny considering what we actually did at the clinic and our unusual clientele.

My muscles strained as I lifted chair after chair, my eyes darting to the clock and counting down the minutes to opening. Suddenly, our work was interrupted by the front door swinging open, causing my heart to lodge itself in my throat.

Has Bree forgotten to lock up? I hoped not because we were so not ready to see patients.

Spinning on my heels, I turned to face the front of the clinic and blew out a sigh of relief when I recognized the man standing in the doorway.

"Ryder, hi!" I exclaimed. "What brings you by?"

Since I'd assisted the local detective in solving my previous vet tech's murder, we had been on great terms. It helped that he was a werewolf and knew about our paranormal patients, because no one could ever have too many friends in the right places.

My gaze traveled down the detective's fit body… all the way to the tiny French bulldog at his feet.

"Oh, you brought Benny," I cooed softly. "How's the sweetest little hellhound baby doing?"

The mermaid and werewolf continued to work, ignoring

Ryder and me, which worked out well because Benny, being the offspring of Hades's dog, was not something we advertised. I was still vague on the details, but from what I'd gathered thus far, hellhound babies were rare. And Ryder had specifically asked me to keep the pup's parentage on the lowdown, so there was that.

I kneeled down to pat Benny between the ears, laughing at the excited, wiggling puppy licking at my wrist.

"Actually, that's why I'm here." Ryder raked his fingers through his tousled brown hair, fixing his piercing green eyes on me. "I need your help. It's important."

Tilting my head, I gazed up at him. Why did I have the feeling that whatever Ryder was about to ask me for was going to make things around here much more interesting?

I stood, brushed the dust from my pants, and rolled my shoulders. If I'd learned anything over the past few months, it was that there was never a dull moment at the Sunny Days Clinic.

Not even when I desperately needed one.

CHAPTER TWO

Always ready to assist, Ryder rolled up his sleeves and joined us in cleaning up the wrecked waiting room. Thanks to his help, we managed to make it mostly presentable, with a few minutes to spare before opening.

Ryder suggested we take Benny for a walk around the block rather than talking where we might be overheard. After a bit of bargaining, Bree agreed to handle things with the mermaid and werewolf, as long as I brought her back a gingerbread latte.

Promising to return soon, I waited for Ryder to leash up Benny and we stepped out into the chilly street.

Walking down Orfus Road, so close to the holidays, was nothing short of magical. Even for someone like me, who didn't celebrate much of anything, I had to appreciate the shift in the air. There was something in the way the world seemed to soften, as if the town itself took a collective breath, letting go of its daily worries for a little while.

Twinkle lights cast a warm, golden glow from shop windows, reflecting off the frost-kissed sidewalks like tiny stars had fallen to earth. The subtle hum of holiday music drifted out of cafes and stores, blending into the soft murmur of people passing by, their laughter and conversation drifting down the street.

The smell of peppermint wafted in the crisp air, mingling with the ever-present hint of pine. That scent was a Bluejay Falls signature—a staple of the season. Every holiday, without fail, the town would be drenched in it, permeating the streets so deeply that you could practically taste the cool, sweet aroma with every breath. When tourists asked about it, the locals always smiled, a twinkle in their eyes, and said it was a Bluejay Falls secret. A tradition.

In reality, the truth was a little more ordinary: the town council had a crew come out to spray the flower arrangements hanging on the lamp posts each morning before dawn with a cedar-and-peppermint scented mist. But perhaps that was the real secret, the way Bluejay Falls took something simple, something mundane, and made it feel magical.

A car honked at a nearby couple as we crossed the street and the two waved at whoever was behind the wheel, shouting their hellos. In front of us, Benny tore toward an unsuspecting bench and attempted to climb it with far too much enthusiasm.

He snarled and growled the entire time, as though he

was battling a mythical dragon and not a collection of wood planks cobbled together. With a playfully annoyed huff, Ryder lifted the dog up so he could sniff at the arm handles before the pup squirmed, requesting to be set back on the sidewalk.

Ryder raised one eyebrow and shot me a bemused glance. "He's certainly peculiar."

As if on cue, Benny pulled on the leash and sprinted down the street, zigging and zagging past sandwich signs and people's legs. Clutching my scarf so it didn't fly away, I jogged after Ryder as he tried to keep up with the hell-hound puppy and apologized to people we body-checked in our path of bulldogged—er, bulldozed—destruction.

My legs pumped as we skirted around the corner, then skidded to a stop as Benny came to an abrupt halt in front of a small bakery with a large bay window. The puppy got up on his hind legs and blew warm breath over the glass, perusing the baked goods displayed in the shop.

"He has great taste," I laughed. "This actually happens to be the same spot Bree wanted me to get her drink from." Bending, I patted the pup on his back. "Good job, Benny."

Still smiling, I straightened and turned toward Ryder. "So, you said you needed my help earlier?"

"Right, yes," the detective said.

Did I notice a glint of mischief in his eyes, or was I imagining things? Before I could dwell on it further, he picked up Benny and gave him a quick scratch behind one ear. Moving inside, he motioned for us to sit down at one of the tables, waiting for me to slip into a seat before he sat down opposite of me.

"It's more of a favor, really," Ryder said.

I blew out a breath, making a loose red curl bounce on my forehead. "Can you be any more vague?" I teased, narrowing my eyes. "What's the favor and why are you acting so strange about it? Oh wait... Is it a werewolf thing? Do you need me to shave something?" His horrified expression had me leaning back in my chair and wheezing with laughter. "Calm down! I'm only kidding. What's the favor?"

"I have to go out of town for a week or so and I was hoping you could watch Benny." Ryder absently stroked the pup's back as he spoke.

My shoulders slumped in relief. For a second, I'd thought Ryder was going to ask me to help him with a case or something equally terrifying.

After my last stint of shoving my nose far where it didn't belong and almost getting killed in the process, I'd had enough police cases to last me a lifetime. Which, for a vamp, was a very, very long time.

Now, watching the world's cutest hellhound baby? That I could do without any problems.

Eyes flicking to the puppy, I put my elbows on the table and rested my chin in my cupped hands. Benny's cute pink tongue darted out, licking Ryder's cheek with a loud slurp.

"Of course," I said. "I'd be happy to help. Are you going on vacation?"

Ryder barked out a laugh. "I wish! I haven't been on vacation in decades. This is a work thing. A case out west."

"You really haven't gone away in that long?" I asked, my brow scrunching. "We need to remedy that."

Had I suggested I take the detective on a vacation?

My skin flushed and my cheeks heated to a temperature that was typically only found at the earth's core. Dropping my gaze to the table, I studied the surface like I suddenly found it unbelievably captivating.

Still avoiding Ryder's eyes, I scratched the back of my neck and mumbled, "So, a case, huh? Anything interesting?"

Whatever it is, it's probably not as fascinating as the idiotic performance you're putting on right now, I cursed myself out in my head and waited for his reply.

Thankfully, the man cleared his throat and spoke, putting me out of my misery. "Nothing exciting. A friend of mine is on the force in another town and they're short staffed. I told him I'd lend a hand with a string of break-ins they've been dealing with. Though I think it's only an excuse to get me out there. Davey comes from a big family and he gets a little sentimental around the holidays. He needs everyone nearby."

"I'm guessing he's a werewolf, huh? Big pack?"

Ryder grinned. "Nope. All human. He's a good guy. I've known him almost my entire life. One of those friends you can't say no to."

I instantly thought of Bree. "I know the type." My gaze landed on Benny, who'd fallen asleep in Ryder's arms.

"How come you don't have a sitter for him? Not that I'm not happy to help out."

"Isn't it obvious?" Ryder asked. "I can't trust anyone with Benny, not with him being a hellhound. I figured since you already know about his little secret and are kind of a genius with animals, this was a good fit. But honestly, if you're too busy, I completely understand."

My hands shot up in surrender. "Oh, no! I would love to have him for as long as you need. And I completely understand," I said. "Speaking of his... situation. As far as his care is concerned, is there anything new I should know about?"

"Nothing out of the ordinary." Ryder shrugged. "He's pretty much a regular dog. Watch out for him sneaking food because he loves to do that. He gets his walks three times a day, but he can survive on two if you can put up with his sulking." He rubbed his temple. "What else? Ah, yes! Watch out for him glowing around people. He's been doing that lately when he gets excited."

I swallowed. "Got it. Treats, walks, glowing. Seems like pretty standard pup care."

"He really is an easy-going little guy," Ryder said, scratching behind Benny's ears. The puppy yawned in response, his tongue lolling out as he fell fast asleep again. "See what I mean? If you do take him for walks though, he loves the dog park down on Fifth and Smitherson. It's his favorite place."

Luckily for Benny, I knew exactly where that was. I even recommended some of our more particular patients take their dogs there, since it seemed to be a real community place. It was large enough to have room for dogs of all sizes, and it had several benches for the owners to relax in the shade while they let their pups play in the off-leash area.

I couldn't wait to take Benny there so I could finally test the place out for myself. It wasn't like I could frequent the park with my own pet: the bat with the attitude problem.

Speaking of whom...

I pushed away from the table to stand up. "Sorry to cut the walk—or nap—short, but I should get back before all my patients show up at once and Bree loses it."

"No luck on hiring a tech replacement yet?" Ryder asked.

"Not at all," I admitted. "It is shockingly hard to find good supernatural assistants if you can believe it."

Ryder cradled Benny like a baby and stood up after me. "I'll keep my ears open for you if I hear of someone looking."

"Don't hold your breath," I joked, then added, "But thank you. So, when do you leave?"

"Tomorrow," he answered. "Is that too soon?"

Mentally checking my growing list of chores and the steady number of patients we had booked at the clinic, I pushed it all out of my head and nodded. "Not at all. I can always bring Benny to the clinic so he can play with Bree. It'll be great."

"Thanks so much for doing this, Lia. I owe you one. Maybe I can pay you back with a vacation one day."

His comment caused me to stumble, and I tripped over the empty table next to ours. Keeping my back to Ryder so I didn't embarrass myself further, I got in line and made small talk while trying not to picture what a vacation with the detective would look like.

The last thing I needed in my life right now was another distraction, no matter how chiseled that distraction's jaw was or how broad his shoulders were. I ordered Bree's latte and got her a snowman cookie as a bonus, then parted ways with Ryder with the promise to meet him after work tomorrow to pick up Benny.

As he walked away, I forced myself not to look after him. The only thing I wanted from the detective was an excuse to play with his adorable hellhound while he was solving cases. Yep. That was all I wanted. Puppy kisses. Nothing else. No mess. No interruptions.

This was the new Ophelia Pane. Her life was simple, and that was the way she liked it.

My smile grew as I made my way down the street and toward the clinic. Life was finally settling down.

CHAPTER THREE

B y the time my shift finished and morning came around, I was beyond exhausted. The last thing I heard before my head hit the pillow was Byrd rustling around in the back of my kitchen cupboards.

Sure enough, I awoke to the sound of an alarm and a torn apart cereal box with tiny wheat donuts sprinkled all over the kitchen floor. Hoping Ryder would be late, I rushed around, quickly tidying both myself and the mess the unrepentant bat had left in his wake.

Ryder was, unsurprisingly, on time. My breath hitched in my lungs as I jogged to answer the knock on my door. Swinging it open wide, I tried to steady my breathing and ushered them inside.

"Sorry to keep you waiting," I said between quick pants. "I must have overslept."

That wasn't entirely untrue, since I had ended up falling asleep again whilst brushing my teeth.

Ryder smiled widely, stacking the bags of doggie goods he dragged with him next to the couch. "No trouble at all. You're sure this is all right?"

"Definitely!" I exclaimed. Scooping Benny up from the floor, I gave him a big squeeze then set him back down so he could explore his home away from home. "I can't wait to spend more time with the little guy."

Over my shoulder, Byrd chittered and hissed when the puppy trotted past him.

I rolled my eyes at Byrd's dramatics. "The bat, however, might need some convincing."

"Oh, Benny loves other animals," Ryder said. "Especially bats. And spiders. And snakes. And birds. Pretty much anything he can chase is a big hit." He studied Byrd, who crouched atop the kitchen cupboards. "Maybe don't let Benny catch him, though. He can get slobbery."

Chuckling, I nodded. "Noted. When are you heading out?"

"In an hour," Ryder replied, checking his watch. "Speaking of which, I didn't get a chance to take Benny out yet. Do you mind running him over to the park?"

"Of course! I took the night off, so I have all the time in the world."

I grabbed Benny's leash and waited for him to make his rounds before stepping out with Ryder. As the detective said his goodbyes to the little hellhound, my heart hitched.

The two really were an adorable pair, and if I was the

kind of woman who happened to be affected by men who had a sweet spot for puppies—which I was, but that was beside the point—I would've been struggling not to melt into a puddle on the floor from the sight. Benny licked Ryder's face two times over before he let his owner walk away, and I swore I saw the detective's eyes glisten when he left.

My chest warmed, and I gave myself a mental slap. No. Personal. Interests.

Clicking the leash onto Benny's collar, I locked up and took off down the road toward the dog park. The one the hellhound frequented wasn't too far from my house, nestled in the more residential area of town. Tucked behind an oak-lined path, the park was an unexpected sliver of green amid the quiet neighborhood. The large space was dotted with towering birch trees that hid it from the main road and gave enough privacy to dogs and their owners that it truly felt like a secret garden for canines.

The park was a cozy spot bordered by a rustic wooden fence with every other slat painted in a fun, bright color, and a welcome sign adorned with paw prints swayed in the wind as I passed beneath it. There were two flower pots on either side of the entry, which held small pine trees that had been decorated to celebrate the wintery season. Benny paused to sniff at them, his nose scrunching. Those were also scented, it appeared.

Inside, the park was split into two sections, one for large breeds and one for smaller ones, then a third isolated area behind a secondary fence for off-leash play. Around the designated walking spaces sat several benches, most of which were already occupied by owners. I spotted a couple taking photos with a chubby golden retriever and had to hold Benny down before he accosted them with his pure joy and excitement.

Around the edges of the park sat several agility courses filled with wooden ramps, long winding tunnels, and posts painted in bright colors for the more athletic canines to jump over. The massive water fountain next to the agility course was covered in snow and appeared to be frozen, but I could imagine how much fun visitors to the park had with it in the summer months. I was willing to bet it became a puppy splash pad.

All in all, I could see why Benny loved this place. It was quite the setup for a dog park.

A tennis ball blew past us, and Benny nearly yanked my arm from its socket as he tore off after it. My boots clambered on the slick ground as I struggled to keep up with the pup as he raced through the park after the bright yellow ball.

"Benny! Slow down!" I yelled, trying to push the hair from my face as the wind ripped it free of my scarf.

My cries fell on deaf ears. And if anything, the words only seemed to propel the tiny dog to run faster. Panic rose in my chest as the park zoomed by in my periphery at a dizzying speed. Was super speed a hellhound ability? I couldn't recall the list Ryder had given me earlier well enough, which only made my anxiety skyrocket. What if

Benny ran so fast he outed himself in front of all these humans?

A protruding tree root caught my boot, and I stumbled forward, catching myself quickly, thanks to my vampire abilities. But not quick enough to stop myself from biting down on my tongue, filling my mouth with the tangy taste of blood.

Fang it! Now I was hungry.

The hellhound snarled and leaped in the air, flying like a superhero in training as he zoomed toward the tennis ball. He caught it, thank the stars, and landed on his paws with a loud thud, snarling as he ripped into the ball like it had offended his ancestors.

I doubled over next to him, resting my elbows on my thighs as my breathing came in short bursts.

"If you want him to obey your commands, you should lower the pitch of your voice."

Startled, I stopped breathing entirely and twisted around to look at the person hovering over me. The woman, in her late thirties, had her arms folded over a wide chest. Her blond hair was tied into such a tight knot it made her eyebrows pull away from her face. Hawk-like blue eyes watched me, inspecting every motion with a disapproving glare.

She reminded me of my intimidating high school gym teacher, and I immediately felt flustered… and slightly terrified she was going to order me to drop and give her twenty push-ups right there in the snow.

The scowl on her face deepened as she watched me

struggle to stand up straight. Benny's leash looped around my ankles and I almost fell on my face several times, trying to escape its confines. Finally, after several uncomfortable seconds, I was able to stand up straight and meet the woman eye to eye.

"Pardon me?" I asked, trying to keep any sign of my high school gym trauma from my tone.

She extended a hand in the same manner I imagined army generals did. "Dana Seller," she said. "I'm a dog trainer who specializes in"—she cast a side glance at Benny —"special cases."

He was special all right.

The woman pulled out a thick tube of lip balm from her back pocket and slathered it over her lips, puckering them at me as she waited for a response.

"Oh," I said sheepishly. "Benny isn't mine. I'm dog sitting him today. But I don't think we need the services. He's usually a very good boy."

Before I could object, Dana grabbed the leash from my hand and yanked it taught. The motion lifted Benny's front paws from the ground and he dropped the tennis ball in a confused huff. His big eyes bulged as he fought against the leash, hind legs burying deeper into the earth. The dog trainer didn't let go, even when Benny growled.

Rage rose through my body. How dare she treat the pup so harshly!

My eyes narrowed to slits, and I swore if I were a cartoon character, I would have had steam billowing from my ears. In this case, I was working hard not to rip the woman's head off. In other words, I was struggling to contain my vampiric strength and all the anger that part of my psyche was blasting outward.

Snatching the leash from her hands, I fixed her with a death glare and said, "Please don't do that again." My gums ached with the longing to let my fangs extend.

Dana gave me a tight-lipped smile. Ignoring my death glare, she reached into her messenger bag and pulled out a stack of business cards and handed me one. I noted the address on the back, a fancy apartment building not far from where my house was. It annoyed me how close I lived to this unbelievably rude woman.

"If you change your mind and would like to train him properly," she said, "give me a call. I work miracles."

"Not my dog," I hissed under my breath at her retreating back. Looking down at Benny, I added, "What was her problem?"

The hellhound cocked his head to the side, huffed out a warm breath that turned to fog in the cool air, then returned to chewing on the tennis ball he'd dropped. His drool had painted the yellow a dark brown and there were tear marks from his teeth all over the felt fabric. Grimacing, I realized whoever owned the ball wouldn't want it back. Shielding my eyes with one hand, I searched the park, trying to find who may have dropped it.

My eyes landed on a pile of them near the off-leash area we'd passed earlier.

Right at the feet of Dana… the sadistic dog trainer.

Had she thrown the tennis ball to test Benny and try to drum up new business? That woman was off her rocker.

Shaking my head, and trying to calm the rage still swirling in my stomach, I walked Benny as far away from her and her line of sight as possible.

We spent twenty minutes testing out the obstacle courses before heading to the small dog area where Benny had a great time chasing another Frenchie around while I chatted with a bookstore owner from the other side of town. All in all, our first outing was a success, if you didn't count the rude interruption before.

As we made our way back home, my coat vibrated, and I pulled my phone from the pocket, my nose scrunching at the name on the screen.

I tapped to answer and brought the phone to my ear. "Bree? Is everything all right at the clinic?"

"All great here, boss," the pixie replied. "But do you think you can pop in for a minute?"

My ears perked. "What's going on?"

"Nothing to worry about. Just come by when you can."

Voices came from the other side of the line, but Bree hung up before I could make out who it was or what was being said. The knot in my belly returned.

Why was she being so cryptic? It wasn't like Bree not to blab every detail of her day, and the lack of information, combined with the mysterious request to come in, had me worried.

I waited for Benny to mark another tree, then pulled him

gently toward the exit. It was beginning to look like I wouldn't get the night off I craved after all.

As we marched out of the park, a new commotion caught my attention. I twisted to look in the direction of Dana, who was no longer alone. There was a short, stout man beside her, and the two appeared to be in the midst of a very heated argument. The man's arms flapped around as he talked, and his long scarf fell to the snow where he stomped over it, his boots leaving muddy marks in the dark wool.

Dana's cheeks puffed in anger, and her jaw worked. I could all but hear the dog trainer's teeth grinding from way over here as she listened to the man rant. In between his outbursts, Dana reapplied her lip balm and her eyes rolled skyward.

"Looks like she pissed off another dog owner, Benny," I told the hellhound with a chuckle.

Unfortunately, Benny cared less for park drama than he did for the garbage truck that drove past us on the road nearby. Using what I was now convinced was his hellhound super speed, he raced in the direction the truck had gone, pulling me along with him. My legs hit the pavement, arms pumping as I sped up.

One thing was for certain: by the time Ryder got his dog back, I would be in the best shape of my vamp life.

CHAPTER FOUR

I arrived at the clinic just in time to catch Bree ushering a client out. The woman had two ferrets, one perched on each of her shoulders, their shiny tails swaying as she moved. Ever the picture of efficiency, Bree handed her a small paper bag filled with a mix of treats, care supplies, and the folder of forms we always sent home with new patients. The woman gave a nod of thanks before disappearing down the street, her ferrets chittering as they nestled closer to her neck.

Bree lingered on the doorstep for a moment, her pixie features glowing in the light of the setting sun. How humans didn't realize she was something paranormal and otherworldly, I'd never know.

Catching sight of me, she turned, and the glint in her eyes warned me of what I was about to face. My stomach dropped, and moving swiftly, I headed toward the door, my heart picking up speed with each step I took.

Since Bree wasn't a vet, we'd had only nail trims, bandage changes, and medication pickups scheduled for the night. It was the reason I'd been able to take the evening off in the first place.

But now, standing on the sidewalk and peering through the large front windows, it was clear the night's plans had taken an abrupt turn.

It wasn't just one or two patients. Not even close. The waiting room was abso-freaking-lutely packed.

From where I stood, I could see two dogs—one a nervous-looking terrier pacing in tight circles, and the other a droopy-eyed hound sprawled across the floor—a gray cat sharpening its claws on one of the chairs, and several small cages stacked on the counter that I assumed held birds, rabbits, or some other adorable pocket-sized creatures.

And that was just what I could see from the street.

This was supposed to have been a quiet, easy night, but from the looks of it, the clinic was only an ornery goat and an angry alpaca away from being a full petting zoo.

Bree held open the door as I hurried to her side. "How did it get so busy?" I whispered. "Give me a second to settle Benny in and I'll get ready to clock in."

"No need," the pixie answered, waving me off.

My brow scrunched in confusion. "Bree, I don't know if you noticed, but that's a lot of patients, and I doubt they're all here for nail trims."

"I know. But I have help."

When she saw the creases in my forehead deepen, she chuckled and nodded for me to step inside. "You'll see. I just wanted your approval before I signed off on this."

If she was trying to ease my anxiety, she was going about this all wrong. Reluctantly, I followed the pixie into the clinic with Benny trotting behind me on his leash.

One by one, Bree spoke to the patients sitting down, letting them know they'd be seen shortly. She grabbed a chart from the stack on top of the reception desk, called out the name, and the woman with the sharp-clawed orange tabby cat stood up. With a warm smile, Bree got her settled in one of the examination rooms before motioning for me to join her in the hallway.

I stepped in close to my pixie tech, already slipping into a clean white lab coat with my name embroidered above the pocket. "You can get another patient settled in the next room while I see this patient. I really don't understand how you plan to handle everyone. What if we get a supernatural walk in?"

Without a word, Bree walked toward the exam room located far from the front of the clinic. She pressed a finger to her mouth, the ominous gesture causing my stomach to flop like a fish on land. Turning the handle, she slowly pushed open the door.

To say I was shocked by the sight that met my wide-eyed gaze would have been an understatement.

Inside the small room, it was nothing short of a circus.

Lying on the exam table with his legs and arms restrained was a well-dressed man in his late forties. His crisp black suit was tarnished with spots of white and orange, where some type of unidentifiable liquid dripped on him from canisters arranged around his body. The smell of herbs and smoke filled the room, stinging my eyes and causing them to water. The fine hair on my arms lifted as energy crackled through the room.

On the table, the man's mouth was wide open, and for the first time since I walked in, I noticed the fangs protruding beneath his lips.

Holy smokes! The guy was a vampire!

With no small amount of effort, I peeled my eyes from the vamp to the woman standing over him. Her curly black hair was tied into a messy ponytail on top of her head, and she had so much of the unruly mane that it seemed to be trying its best to break free from its elastic prison. Wispy curls shot out every which way, framing the woman's angled face in the darkness.

Her KHOL-lined green eyes flicked to me briefly, and she gave me a faint smile before biting her lip and focusing on the vampire. She whispered a few words, and as she spoke, the floating canisters poured more of the liquid onto his body.

The woman leaned in, asking, "Ready?"

When the vamp nodded, she tightened a dental clamp over his left fang and, with a sharp twist, yanked it right out of his mouth. The vamp's head lolled backward, a sigh of relief falling from his lips.

"Thank you," he said, the words coming out mumbled.

Was I seeing things? I had never seen a vampire allow anyone to come close to their fangs, let alone thank someone for ripping one out. This was unprecedented behavior and straight up madness.

It was…

My eyes focused on the canisters.

Magic.

"Um, Bree," I said, proud my words came out calmer than I felt. "Care to explain?"

"Lia, meet Grennich. Grennich, meet Dr. Ophelia Pane, and hopefully, your new boss."

Grennich walked around the table and extended a hand. "Pleasure to meet you," she said in a soft, melodic voice. "Skeeter has told me a lot about you."

"You're Skeeter Kraus's friend?"

After the relaxed one-fanged vamp on the table, this was the second most shocking revelation of my evening.

I hadn't realized Skeeter had any friends other than me since he kept to himself for the most part. Trolls were notorious for being loners, and Skeeter's job as a cryptologist made him even more so, since he spent most of his time alone on the computer or poring over old documents. It was what had made us friends in the first place—our lack of social lives outside each other. Up until that moment, I had never heard him so much as mention someone else. Yet here was Grennich… which led me to wondering what exactly she was. Not a mermaid, troll, pixie, or vamp. Maybe a mage?

As if reading my mind, she flashed her teeth and gave me a wide grin. "I'm a fae; I've known that troll since high school," she said. "We go back a long time. He mentioned you were hiring and looking for someone who knew their way around the supernatural world, so I thought I'd stop by. I hope I haven't overstepped and caused too much trouble. Bree seemed like she needed the help."

"What is your experience?" I asked, appreciative of the help but not happy at the idea of any Tom, Dick, or Harry just walking into my clinic and practicing medicine without the proper credentials.

"I'm a licensed veterinarian, although I had to return home to help my village right after graduation, so I haven't worked in a clinic yet," Grennich admitted. "I've also studied with the best healer faes in my village growing up, so I know about every supernatural ailment there is out there. Paranormals of all kinds come to me for help they can't get elsewhere on account of, well, the risk of exposing what they are." She glanced back at the vampire, who was in a delirium of happiness. "Like Mr. Tront, for example. He's had a dead fang for weeks."

I stepped around her to check on the vampire. "How do you feel now, sir?"

"Are you kidding? Fantastic!" he exclaimed. "Grennich, dear, you're a miracle worker. And you say the fang will grow back in a month?"

"Give or take," the fae replied. "I'll send you home with a potion to speed up the healing."

My eyes danced between her and the vamp, unable to

look away. The last time we had a vampire come in with a toothache, it had taken us four hours to get him calm enough to sedate. And even then, he'd fought us tooth and nail—every pun intended. For Grennich to remove a dead fang successfully, by herself in a matter of seconds, was nothing short of a miracle. I knew magic was involved, but still, it was impressive.

I bit the inside of my cheek, ruminating. Skeeter was a solid troll whose opinion I trusted. If he'd sent her my way, it was for a reason.

"Do you mind if I have a quick chat with Bree?" I asked the fae.

"Take all the time you need," she replied. "I need a moment to get Mr. Tront's potion ready, anyway."

Leaving the fae and vampire behind, I stepped out of the room and waited until Bree joined me to close the door behind us. We skirted around the corner and into the small kitchenette, Bree moving for the coffee maker immediately. As she poured herself a steaming mug, I tried to think of reasons why Grennich would not be a good fit.

The only thing I could think of was her lack of experience practicing as a veterinarian, which I had to admit was a problem. She had the knowledge and the initiative to jump in and get the job done, but she'd need help adjusting to working with patients of the non-supernatural variety.

"She could take care of the supernatural clients while you and I handle everyone else," Bree said, making me wonder if everyone could read my mind now or if my poker face really was as bad as I'd been told.

"It's like you're in my head sometimes," I chuckled. "I was just thinking about that. So you like her?"

"Grennich seems great. And she handled that vampire much better than we could have. I really think she would be a good fit."

"Plus she knows Skeeter," I added.

Bree nodded. "Exactly."

"You think she'd mind taking care of paperwork when she's not with patients?" I asked. "We don't get as many supernatural visits, and when she isn't shadowing me to learn more about treating patients, I could use someone to help with the administration side of things around here. Once she is comfortable seeing all types of patients, we could look into hiring another vet tech, especially if we keep growing at our current rate."

"I'm sure she'd be up for it," Bree said. "For what it's worth, she strikes me as someone who truly wants to help people. And healer fae are incredibly powerful. She could be helpful in other areas too. We simply have to be careful she doesn't use her magic out in the open."

I watched Bree gulp down her coffee as fast as possible so she could return to the patients waiting to be seen. My pulse raced, but this time, it was from excitement. Grennich was a gamble, and yet I somehow knew that she would work out.

From the second I'd stepped foot in that examination room, our little team at Sunny Days Clinic felt complete, as though we had found the missing puzzle piece. Perhaps I would come to regret it in the future, but for now, I knew what I had to do.

I looked at Bree, my shoulders slumping with relief. "Looks like we have a new veterinarian."

A vampire, a pixie, and a fae. Now *that* was a team I could get behind.

CHAPTER FIVE

"Benny! Watch out!" I yelped, sliding across the hardwood floors on my socks as I chased after him.

The pup skidded into the tall, wobbly bookshelf in my bedroom. Arms outstretched, I caught the unstable shelf before it toppled over onto Benny. Books fell from the overhead shelves, raining down on my head, and the corner of one beautiful hardcover slammed against my forehead with enough force to make me see stars. Shaking off the blinding pain, I tried to blink my blurry vision back into focus.

After pushing the shelf back to its right position, I made sure it was secure, then turned to face the puppy on the bed. Benny's hind legs stuck out from under a pile of unfolded laundry, and he whimpered as I approached.

"It's all right, buddy." I gently patted the lump on the

bed. "It's safe to come out now. But you have to be more careful where you dig around."

I should've puppy-proofed my house better. How many owners had I walked through a list of things they needed to do before bringing their four-legged bundle of joy home?

Yep. I'd thought I had everything handled, but I hadn't considered the teeny tiny fact that Benny wasn't exactly a regular dog. His baby body may have been small, yet his hellhound powers were growing rapidly, giving him the strength of a dog five times his size.

I made a mental note to tell Ryder about the incident so he could secure his furniture to the walls. We wouldn't want the poor dog getting stuck under something while playing.

Eyeing the lumpy pile, I reached over to my nightstand, where I'd stashed a few doggy treats, and pulled some out. The smell immediately got Benny's attention. With a little growl, the pup emerged from beneath the clothes. His tongue lolled out of the side of his drooling mouth as he sniffed the air for the treats.

Chuckling, I gave him one.

Benny inhaled the snack before I could blink. His head cocked to one side, waiting for my next move.

How could puppies be this ridiculously cute?

If I wasn't careful, I was going to end up with puppy fever, and I certainly didn't have time to be a full-time dog mom... not yet, anyway.

"You're pretty bored, aren't you?"

The dog didn't reply, because, well, he was a dog.

Instead, he nuzzled his wet, treat-covered nose in the palm of my hand and gave another soft whine.

"I'll take that as a yes." I leaned down and placed a kiss on the top of his head. "We should have brought Byrd home with us tonight."

Checking the clock on the wall, I noted how late it was and glanced out the window. The moon was already high in the sky. As both a vampire and someone who worked third shift, I preferred to stay awake through the night, but I'd been hoping to hop in bed a little earlier than usual. I wanted to be at the clinic several hours before we opened, since it was Grennich's first official day, and we needed to start her training.

But with Benny this energetic, there wasn't likely to be any sleeping for me unless I could find a way to tire him out.

My eyes rounded as an idea popped into my head. The dog park was always open, and there wouldn't be anyone there this late at night. Benny could run around and cause all the hellhound chaos he wanted with no one there to witness it. It was a perfect plan!

Jumping off the bed, I yanked the bag of treats off the nightstand. I shoved them into my back pocket and patted my thigh, motioning for Benny to join me. The pup didn't understand where we were going, but he was always ready for an adventure and eagerly trotted behind me.

At the front door, I attached his leash, and we stepped out into the cold night air.

"What do you say, Benny?" I asked the pup. "Ready to get wild—"

Benny was already halfway down the block and pulling me behind him before I could finish the sentence.

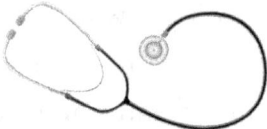

THE DOG PARK felt completely different at night, almost as though we were stepping into a different universe or a horror movie—one where I was pretty sure I'd be the first to die thanks to tripping over my own feet.

Although, as a vampire, I was more likely to be the killer than the victim. But if I was the monster, why did a shiver that had nothing to do with the frigid breeze run down my spine as we stepped through the gate?

Gone was the cheerful playground of the daytime. Now, with darkness hanging around like a heavy cloak and the shadows stretching across the ground as far as they could reach, the place felt more like the set of a low-budget thriller. To top it off, while I was busy wrangling Benny in my house, it had snowed, covering the park in an eerie, glowing white blanket. And although I didn't sense the presence of a single living thing in the area, every instinct in my body screamed that we needed to do our business and get home, ASAP!

"Let's make this a quick one, okay?" I tugged Benny's leash with all the determination of someone who'd prefer being in her bed, cuddled under ten blankets with a mug of hot cocoa rather than having icicles forming on her fangs.

Benny, of course, cared exactly zero percent about my preferences and launched into a full-on sprint, snapping the leash taut when I refused to budge. His tiny paws churned up slushy snow, spraying icy confetti all over my legs as we played some type of twisted tug-of-war. Unable to get his attention or distract him, my patience grew thin as my jeans grew soaked.

It was clear this was going to be a very long night.

Scooping up the wiggling, protesting pup, I headed toward one of the empty fenced-in areas. The moment I unclipped his leash and set him on the ground, he took off as though fired from a cannon. It didn't take long before the foreboding vibes that had put a damper on my mood faded, and I grinned as I chased the eager puppy.

We ran circles around the creepy park, climbing every doggy walkway at least twice. After about twenty minutes of the type of torturous exercise no one in their right mind asks for, Benny finally settled down to do his business on a nearby tree.

Leaning on the fence that encircled the park, I took a moment to catch my breath. I pulled out my phone while I waited for Benny to finish and cleaned up my email's inbox. When had I signed up for so many newsletters?

"Huh." I clicked open an email that Ryder had sent a few hours ago. "Your dad got in safe and sound. He says not to give you treats after midnight or you get too excited," I told the pup. "That would have been good to know before

I gave you a bunch of treats. You aren't going to start terror-izing the town like something from an old movie, are you?"

Benny ignored me, continuing to sniff around the tree.

Laughing at my own sad joke, I looked back down at my phone and worked my way through the string of email notifications. There were several from Bree wishing me luck training Grennich tomorrow and telling me she was excited about the future of our newest recruit.

I had to hand it to Skeeter. He sure had saved the day. I had a feeling the fae was going to be exactly what the clinic needed. Especially with the influx of supernatural patients we'd been getting over the past few months.

A low growl jerked my attention away from the screen and back to Benny. His legs were buried so deep into the snow that I couldn't see his paws anymore, and the tiny hellhound's fur was raised. Every muscle in his back and legs flexed as he stared unblinking at something in the distance.

I squinted into the darkness, seeing nothing.

"What is it, buddy?" I asked. "A squirrel?"

Benny snarled and darted forward toward whatever had captured his attention. I rushed after him, my stomach tightening at the growing distance between us and the exit. It wasn't that I was afraid, but everyone knew that nothing good ever lurked in the bushes this late at night. The last thing I needed was to wrestle with a wayward shifter—or worse, a serial killer—right now.

Trying to watch where I placed each boot, so I didn't step in a pile of dog poop, I followed the pup on a mission as he led us through a stand of trees. The woods weren't thick, and moments later, we emerged on the other side.

Instantly, my nose wrinkled and my eyes watered from the horrific acidic smell that hung heavy in the air. It was almost like someone had set off a smoke bomb.

Next to me, Benny sputtered, alternating between licking his wet snout and rubbing it against his front paws.

"Disgusting! You smell it too, huh?" I asked, pushing the fabric of my scarf over my nose and mouth in what proved to be a futile attempt at escaping the odor. "But what is it?"

It likely wouldn't have been as strong or as horrible to a human, but my vamp senses were going into overdrive from the wretched aroma. I all but smothered myself with my scarf, wrapping it tight enough around my neck to nearly cut off my air almost entirely.

Reluctantly, I followed Benny as he continued the trek into the darkness that seemed to engulf us. He remained focused on his pursuit, and before I knew it, we ended up in a small clearing that I hadn't noticed during our daytime visit.

My gaze scanned the area. I imagined it was actually kind of peaceful when bathed in sunlight.

The quiet of the night was broken when Benny began to bark and dig frantically at something beneath the single pine tree that stood in the center of the clearing. I stepped forward, clicking the leash back onto his collar and trying to pull him away, but he ignored me, barking incessantly as his paws tore at the ground.

A moment later, his teeth sank into something, and panic clawed its way up my throat. "Benny, no! Whatever that is, don't eat it!"

What if we'd stumbled on some hidden party area for college students and the poor little guy found something they'd left behind? What if he ingested something that hurt him? What if—

I bent, prepared to force him to give up whatever he'd found, but I froze, sucking in a cold, ruthless breath as I stared in horror at what Benny had dug up. My mind stopped working, and my lips parted, but no sound came out.

Satisfied with his discovery, the hellhound backed away from the tree and proudly pranced over to stand still beside me. His head swiveled to look between me and the body he'd unearthed.

My stomach turned.

Step by shaky step, I drew closer to the person lying horribly still in the snow. The hair on the back of my neck stood on edge, and I struggled to breathe thanks to the bile rising in my chest.

I swallowed hard, my pulse hammering away with the intensity of a power tool. "Is... Is that the dog trainer?"

There was no mistaking Dana Seller's motionless, dead body. The dog trainer's eyes were wide open and staring into nothingness, and she wore the same clothing she had when I'd met her before. Other than her being quite obviously gone, she appeared to be completely unharmed. No blood. No signs of a struggle. It was so strange.

Scanning the surrounding ground, I noticed her purse lying on top of a cut-down tree. The contents were scattered all around the leather satchel. My gaze caught on Dana's lip balm, and my heart gave an unexpected jolt at the realization she'd never use it again.

I was so involved in the scene in front of me I didn't even notice Benny had begun sniffing around the body. The hellhound was so close to the dead trainer that I could see his drool landing on her cheek. With a shriek, I leaped forward, scooped him into my arms, then turned and bolted away from the scene.

When I'd put enough distance between us and the lifeless body, I sat Benny down, keeping him snug between my legs. Summoning every shred of mental fortitude I possessed, I forced myself to calm down before pulling my phone from my pocket.

I stared down into Benny's soulful eyes and whispered, "I think we need to wake up your dad."

CHAPTER SIX

R
yder had answered my call on the second ring, and even though he'd been asleep, he'd taken charge of the situation. Hanging up on me, he'd called the station to report what I had told him. Minutes later, he'd called me back, letting me know backup was on the way and doing his best to calm my panic.

I would've preferred Ryder to be there in person to handle things, but he assured me everything would be fine, and although the officer handling his cases was a junior hire, he was capable.

But I was beginning to question Ryder's assessment as I watched the hot mess express train wreck that was unfolding in front of me. This cop was inexperienced when it came to handling serious crimes and it definitely showed.

Bright lights flashed and reflected on the snow from the

officer's police cruiser, making the park look more like a happy carnival and less like a grim crime scene. If not for the abundance of yellow tape sectioning off the clearing we'd found Dana's body in, passersby would probably have thought there was a late-night party happening.

I couldn't hide my cringe as the young uniformed man tripped over the crime scene investigator's bag on the ground. He regained his footing and turned, raking bony fingers through his ashy brown hair as he glared down at the bag. His hazel eyes narrowed, and the thin mustache above his lip twitched in annoyance. Despite the distance between me and the crime scene, it was obvious the officer was in way over his head. Heck, even his uniform seemed to be too large for his frame, as though he'd borrowed it for the day.

Catching me staring, he tipped a large-brimmed hat at the coroner and shuffled his feet in my direction. The weather had warmed considerably and whatever snow was in the clearing had begun to melt, staining the officer's gray slacks in dark spots. He stepped around a slushy pile with all the grace and agility of a pig on roller skates, adding to the muck covering his uniform. Whoever he'd borrowed it from wasn't going to be happy...

My chest tightened as he approached. What if he assumed I was the killer and decided to take me in? Who would watch Benny until Ryder returned to save both of us?

"You're free to go, Miss Pane," the officer said.

I blew out the breath I'd been holding. "Are you sure? You don't want to ask me any questions?"

Sure, I wanted to be presumed innocent unless proven guilty, but didn't he need to ask at least one or two questions after viewing the scene to make sure I wasn't a raving mad serial killer?

At my feet, Benny whined. See? Even the dog knew the officer wasn't following protocol in the slightest.

"No need," the officer replied, putting his hands in his front pockets and rocking back on his heels. "It's pretty clear what happened here tonight."

Was it? I wasn't so sure, and I'd been at the park a lot longer than he had. How could it be obvious if he'd been at the scene for less than a half hour and had barely glanced in Dana's direction?

The only thing that seemed clear to me was the officer was either a savant at solving crimes… or he was stupid.

Utterly baffled, I rose on my tiptoes to look over his shoulder toward the crime scene. "So what happened?"

"I'm sorry. I'm not at liberty to divulge that information."

Oh, so now he wanted to follow protocol. "What about the man I saw her arguing with before?" I asked, unable to help myself.

"Nothing to note there." The officer waved me off dismissively. "We already spoke to Mrs. Seller's husband—I mean, her *ex*-husband—and he confirmed it was a simple disagreement."

It hadn't looked like a disagreement to me. They'd been fighting. Hard. Plus, wasn't the spouse, or ex-spouse, always the main person of interest? I wanted to tell the officer that, but he seemed to have already moved on.

He reached into his pocket and pulled out a business card with the Bluejay Falls Police emblem on the front. The back of the card had his name printed on it: Archie Baggard, Patrol Officer.

Archie handed me the card with a grin. "If you think of anything that might be pertinent, give me a call."

He walked away before I could reply. In my hands, the card crinkled as I closed my fist around it, confusion setting in.

My gaze dropped to meet Benny's. "Well, that's the end of that, I suppose," I told the pup. "Quite the eventful night, huh? We should probably get you home to bed."

With that, I turned and headed toward the entrance, relieved to put more distance between Dana's lifeless body and myself. It was in the officer's hands now.

This isn't my problem to solve, I told myself.

But as I marched down the street toward my house, I couldn't shake the feeling that something was off. My shoulders hunched.

"Don't do it," I mumbled out loud, earning me a confused look from the pup at my feet.

I was absolutely going to stay out of whatever happened to the poor dog trainer if it was the last thing I did. Not to mention I had more than enough to deal with as it was. The police would handle it.

Besides, who wanted to chase dead ends when there was sleep to be had?

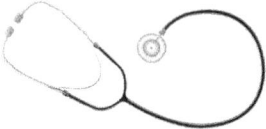

THE COFFEE MACHINE sputtered to life in the corner of the kitchenette, filling the entire space with the fragrance of nutmeg and frothed milk. I inhaled the scent, reaching for the box of Crimson Quench as I watched Bree fill two large mugs of coffee for her and Grennich. She handed one to the fae, who sprinkled a finely ground powder on hers, then mixed it with a little spoon.

Grennich caught me looking and grinned. "Sweetener. I have a sugar allergy."

My cheeks warmed with embarrassment. "I thought you were adding a little spell to yours."

"Oh, I am!" Grennich winked. "But it doubles as a sweetener." She glanced at the blood juice box in my hand. "You know I can spell that to taste like coffee for you, right?"

If my eyes could jump out of my head, do a lap around the kitchen, then pop back in again, they would have done so.

"Where have you been all my life?" I asked the fae, still staring at her in disbelief.

"Mostly New Jersey."

Next to me, Bree's laugh turned to wheezing as she

choked on her coffee. All three of us dissolved into giggles and my chest filled with a warm, contented glow.

Grennich had only been working at the clinic for a few hours, but it already felt like she belonged here. She was the perfect fit for Sunny Days Animal Clinic. We had our team.

My heart gave a painful squeeze as the memory of Justin, our vet tech who'd passed away, flashed through my mind. Hopefully, we could keep our team intact this time.

"Did you two hear about the dog trainer?" Grennich asked, sipping her coffee.

In an instant, the blood in my mouth had soured. "Um, Dana Seller?"

"I think that's her name." The fae's eyebrows drew together. "Apparently, she was found dead in the dog park last night. Ironic."

Reaching out, I gripped the counter, holding myself steady. I'd been trying to put the nightmare of finding Dana behind me by focusing on work. But now the fear, confusion, and sadness for a life lost—even one that I hadn't particularly taken a shine to during our one meeting—came rushing back.

Our town was small and news traveled fast around here, sure, but it had been less than twelve hours since Benny had dug up the clearing, and people were already talking. How they got the information was beyond me because I'd checked the online paper this morning and there was nothing mentioned about Dana or the park.

What if the town found out that Benny and I had been there? I knew exactly what would happen: people would make excuses to stop by, hoping to get a bit more gossip. We were busy enough as it was. The last thing I needed was half the town loitering in my clinic's lobby while I was trying to care for my patients.

My forehead creased with worry. "How did you hear about it?"

"A friend who runs the yarn store on Acorn Avenue called me. She found out because Dana was her neighbor's dog trainer."

"I heard some of the patients talking about it," Bree added. "The cops said she choked on something. What a horrible way to go."

That couldn't be right. My mind spun as I recalled the scene from last night, unable to remember any signs that Dana had choked to death. Where had the police gotten that idea? However Archie had come to that conclusion, it wasn't from something they'd discovered in the clearing.

Perhaps they'd found something during her autopsy? I looked at my watch. It would have to be the fastest autopsy ever completed if the police had it cleared within hours. While unlikely, it wasn't impossible.

My bones creaked as I shifted positions, my stomach aching from tension. Why was I so anxious? I had done nothing wrong, so why was the situation bothering me so much?

Because the cause of death is wrong and you know it. The words flashed in my mind like a neon sign.

But what if they'd missed something and it led the investigation in the wrong direction?

55

Do not do it...

Ignoring my inner voice's warning, I pushed away from the counter and tossed the Crimson Quench in the trash can.

"Be right back." Sneaking past the two, I made my way down the corridor toward the waiting room.

While I'd have liked to relax, I couldn't get what Grennich had said out of my mind. I needed to find out how the police knew Dana had died from choking, especially since I didn't believe that to be the case.

I had no proof, of course. All I had was a nagging sense that something was amiss at the scene of the crime and I had to let Officer Baggard know what I suspected.

Pulling out his business card, I flattened it out on the check-in desk and dialed the number. The line rang once, and he instantly answered. I bit down on my tongue at the sound of the officer's high-pitched voice on the other end.

"Officer Baggard here."

"Hi, there." I tugged at the collar of my lab coat awkwardly. "This is Ophelia Pane."

A long silence stretched between us, followed by the officer's footsteps echoing over the phone line. A door closed on his end and he cleared his throat loud enough to make my eardrums pop.

"Yes, hello. How did you get my phone number?"

"You gave me your card." I tried to keep my eyes from rolling to the back of my head. Who's bright idea had it been to leave this man in charge? "At the crime scene last night. I was the one who found Dana Seller."

"Right, yes. Sorry, Miss Pane. It has been quite the day here, as I'm sure you can imagine."

Chasing false leads would do that to you.

"That was why I called." I frowned, tapping the end of a pen on the desk. "I heard the police are labeling the death as accidental because of a choking hazard, but you know how this town loves to spin tall tales, so I wanted to double check if that was truly the case." I paused, then added, "Especially since there was nothing at the scene to signify she'd choked."

"Where did you hear about our findings?"

"O-Oh, from here and there," I stammered. "Am I wrong?"

Was it me, or did the officer groan on the other line?

"Look, Miss Pane, I have heard about your involvement with Officer Wolff's last case, but I will have you know I do not need, nor want, a civilian meddling with my investigation," he said sternly. "And no, you are not wrong. If it would put your mind at ease, we found sufficient evidence to satisfy my conclusion. A peanut lodged in Mrs. Seller's throat. Now, if you'll excuse me, I have more urgent matters demanding my attention."

"Are you absolutely sure? Because when I—"

"Miss Pane," the officer interrupted. "Please leave the police work for the professionals and go pet puppies and kittens, or whatever it is that you vets do all day. You have yourself a good evening."

As before, he dismissed me without another word. The line went dead, leaving me clenching the phone and listening to the dial tone. Grinding my fangs in annoyance, I slammed down the phone with a frustrated snarl. I wasn't truly upset with Officer Baggard for dismissing me so abruptly—heck! he had every right to since I was a civilian sticking my nose in where it didn't belong—I was mad because I knew I was right.

I couldn't tell you why, but that little voice inside that usually guided me in the right direction told me there was no way Dana Seller had choked on a peanut in the middle of the dog park.

Still seething, I pulled my cell phone from my pocket and typed out a text to Ryder. Perhaps he'd have better luck at changing the officer's mind, considering his high standing at the station. Somehow, I doubted it, but it was worth a shot.

Squaring my shoulders, I walked to the front door and flipped the sign to open. As I unlocked the door, I couldn't help but scan the dark street. My fangs popped out on instinct at the sense of danger that wasn't there. I rolled my eyes and forced them to retract before I accidentally scared a human client.

I watched one of our regular clients make her way down the street with two carriers in tow. My obsession with the dead trainer would have to wait, because I had patients who needed my full attention.

Shrieks and meows echoed down the dark street. I narrowed my eyes, trying to peer into the crates that either held two furious cats or two hangry chupacabras.

As the woman neared, two pairs of glowing red eyes stared back at me. Chupacabras it was.

Remembering Officer Baggard's words, I barely swallowed back a snort.

Go pet some kittens?

If he only knew...

CHAPTER SEVEN

My shift ended with the same chaotic energy it had started with. There were three pee accidents, one dog fight to break up thanks to an owner not obeying our leash rules, two dachshunds sneakily ripping open bags of food on our product shelves while their moms gossiped, and one cat who'd been hit by a car. The kitty had needed a two-hour surgery to repair the damage done to its back leg, but it had gone well and my patient was going to be just fine.

By the time the sun rose and I locked up, all I could think of was crawling under a blanket and staying there for the rest of eternity.

"That was fun," Grennich said from beside me. Behind her, Bree zipped up a bright pink coat and wrapped a glittery purple scarf around her neck.

I eyed the fae suspiciously. "You have an odd definition of what the word 'fun' means."

"No, really," she insisted, holding out Bree's sparkly purse for the pixie to take. "For a first day, I got a good amount of training. And the patients were all lovely."

"Even the troll with the attitude?" Bree asked, raising an eyebrow in curiosity.

Grennich waved her hand dismissively. "Harry? Oh, he's completely harmless. Turns out he's just lactose intolerant, poor thing. It's been messing with his sleep, and well, we all know how cranky everyone gets with no sleep. Once we switch up his diet, he'll be a lot less grumpy, I'm sure of it."

There was a softness in the way Grennich spoke about the troll, like she genuinely cared for her patients, no matter how large or scary they were. The twinkle in her eyes as she talked about him had some of the tension in my shoulders seeping away. Witnessing such a level of enthusiasm for her work on the very first day—without even a trace of panic or an urge to bolt from our supernatural patients—was an intense relief. Hiring Grennich felt like one of the best decisions I'd made.

I glanced over at Bree, who had been nodding along excitedly, her expression filled with approval. Maybe it was because Bree had worked at Sunny Days long enough to be familiar with the stress and high demands of caring for supernatural creatures.

Grennich's enthusiasm gave me hope that once she was

fully trained, the clinic might finally be in safe hands when I took a day off.

"Want to grab a coffee before heading home?" Bree asked the fae. Her eyes darted to me briefly. "I'm assuming you're going to get Benny and Byrd settled in for the weekend?"

I patted the carrier bag I held, the bat sleeping snuggly in a mountain of blankets inside. "Yep! I can't wait to get these boots off and relax for a while. After I walk Benny, of course."

Saying our goodbyes, I double-checked the locks, tucked Byrd's carrier case under my arm, and headed for home. My home wasn't too far from the clinic, although the icy roads made for a slog of a drive; it took twice as long as usual to make the trek.

The moment I unclipped Benny's leash, the hellhound tore around the house with the speed of... well, a hellhound. He ran circles around me, barking at Byrd's carrier. Inside, the bat chattered in disdain, his hisses echoing through my living room.

I refreshed Benny's water bowl and busied him with a snack while I got Byrd settled in the laundry room—the bat's favorite spot in the house. I hadn't even closed the door behind me before I heard him scurry out of the carrier and into the laundry basket, where he no doubt burrowed his way into the center of the freshly washed towels.

Shaking my head and smiling, I made a mental note to rewash that load later.

After letting Benny go wild in the backyard—because

there was no way I was going back to the dog park again—I settled in on the couch, my body half buried under the world's largest blanket. Clutching a cold Crimson Quench in one hand, I reached for the remote with the other, eager to turn on a movie to fall asleep to. On the opposite wall, a light breeze drifted in through the open bay window and I sighed in delight at the combination of coolness on my face and the warmth of the heating pad built into the blanket.

I'd made it an entire two minutes into a rom-com when a loud screech pierced the air. The blood box jumped out of my hand, landing on the carpet in a horrific splash of red that was absolutely going to leave a stain.

Heart racing, I leaped from the couch and rushed toward the sound that seemed to be coming from my bedroom. My feet skidded across the hardwood floor as I ran down the narrow hallway leading to the rear of the house. I rushed into the room, eyes wide with terror and barely feeling pain as my shoulder slammed into the doorframe.

"What happened here?" I yelled, my eyes scanning the disaster strewn out before me. Clothes were scattered all over the bed and floor, and the lamp on the nightstand had been turned over and fallen to the floor. A wet stain covered a large section of my duvet. I wasn't sure I wanted to know where it had come from.

Amidst the chaos sat Benny. Drool dripped from his panting mouth, and his gaze was fixated on something rustling around in the closet. With a groan, I closed my eyes and counted to ten.

When my pulse finally slowed, I walked toward the closet doors. Sucking in a deep breath, I opened them wide. As soon as I did, Byrd's small body fluttered past me, his wings brushing my cheek and neck as he made his escape. Benny was on his tracks instantly.

"Guys! Stop it!"

Without a second thought, I gave chase after the two troublemakers. They cleared the distance between the bedroom and the front of the house in a matter of seconds, and while I did my best to keep up; the rascals were running on batteries I didn't have. My body was exhausted from the night's shift.

For a moment, I considered using my bat speed—which I was yet to master, much to the dismay of my mother—but just thinking about it gave me hives. Still, I picked up my pace when another crash sounded from the living room.

Benny's frantic barking filled the house, then grew softer.

"Benny?" I shouted, my panic causing my voice to rise.

There was no answer. When I reached the living room, my body stilled and a wave of terror blurred my vision.

I'd completely forgotten about the open window. The curtains flapped in the wind and there was a Benny-shaped hole in the window's screen. A normal Frenchie wouldn't have been able to leap up so high, but Benny wasn't normal.

Peering outside, I saw Benny's body getting smaller as he chased a flying Byrd down the street.

The bat could have gotten far out of the pup's reach, but

he was flying just high enough to taunt Benny. Were all bats jerks, or just the one who'd adopted me?

Cursing under my breath, I threw on my coat and ran out the door. Following Benny's echoing snorts, I quickly caught up with the naughty dog. I was beginning to inch close enough to grab him when he made a sharp right turn.

My breath hitched and my lungs ached from the cold air as I did my best to keep up with the pup. In a less than graceful move, I careened around the corner, running across the street and nearly colliding with a parked car.

Glancing up, I spotted Byrd as he disappeared into the cover of a thick pine tree on the street corner. As expected, Benny took position under said tree and continued to bark incessantly for the bat to emerge.

Seizing the opportunity, I clipped the leash on his collar before doubling over as I fought to catch my breath.

"He's not coming down," I said between ragged breaths. "Let's go home. Byrd knows his way back; he's not a pet, and this isn't his sightseeing trip. You, however, aren't supposed to be running around without a chaperone."

As I gently tugged to pull Benny away from the tree, the dark shape of a man in my periphery caught my attention. I turned, realizing for the first time where I was. Somehow, with all the running, I had ended up right in front of Dana Seller's apartment building.

The rotating glass doors of the building spun, and I followed the figure as he left the premises, shooting glances all around him as he walked.

I squinted. Something about the man seemed familiar.

He moved oddly, like he was in a hurry, but didn't want to draw attention by jogging. And the way his face was buried in a long scarf made it appear like he was trying to stay out of sight. The man skirted around the side of the building and disappeared from my view, leaving only doubt behind.

"No bloody way," I whispered. "That was him! Dana's ex-husband!"

It had taken me a moment to realize where I'd seen him before, but there was no mistaking it; it was the same man I'd seen the dog trainer arguing with at the park. The scarf had been a dead giveaway.

My jaw clenched, and pulling out my phone, I started to dial Officer Baggard's number. But the phone leaped from my hands when a soft furry paw slammed into my legs and the phone flew.

I looked between Benny and the phone that laid in the slushy snow on the sidewalk. "Was that really necessary?"

The hellhound wagged his whole butt in excitement. Shaking my head, I bent down and retrieved my phone. My eyes flashed to the number I hadn't called yet, then back to Benny. Perhaps the pup was right. Not that I believed Benny had knocked the phone from my hands on purpose, but it may have been for the best that I didn't finish the call.

So far, the junior officer had been anything but agreeable to hearing my thoughts on Dana's case. Telling him I'd seen the ex-husband acting suspicious wasn't likely to go the way I wanted it to. If anything, it would only make me appear like a stalker who had nothing better to do than hang around a dead woman's apartment building.

If I wanted Officer Baggard to listen to me, I needed to bring him irrefutable proof that Dana's death was not accidental. A knot formed in my throat. I swallowed it down, ignoring the alarm bells going off in my head. It appeared I'd have to get involved in the case after all—for the sake of the truth, that was.

Fingers crossed I could give the police what they needed without getting into trouble this time. I thought about the last time I'd injected myself into an active police case. Maybe it was best to cross my toes as well.

CHAPTER EIGHT

I t was beginning to look like I'd let my ego get the best of me. The initial search for Dana's ex-husband yielded zero results. In fact, I was even more confused about the woman's life than I had been before I'd opened up my laptop and began my search.

According to Dana's website and social media profiles, she had never been married, and she currently lived on her own in a completely different town. No mention of Bluejay Falls came up in connection to her name no matter how deeply I spiraled into the abyss of the internet.

How strange.

I checked a few more places and finally came across the address for Dana's current apartment building on a website promoting dog training services for various companies. There was nothing to be found on her ex, though.

How was I supposed to get the information to nudge

Officer Baggard in the right direction in this case if I couldn't even find a simple name online? It was beyond infuriating.

Grunting, I shut the laptop and slid it across the couch with a bit more force than was necessary. At the other end, Benny drowsily opened one eyelid to see what the commotion was before returning to his nap.

"Lucky pup! I'd kill for some sleep right about now." I winced as the words left my lips.

Perhaps it was best not to think about killing at this particular moment.

My eyes rounded as an idea popped into my head. I might have been completely useless at online sleuthing, but I knew someone whose entire job revolved around that type of stuff.

With renewed hope, I leaped off the couch. Grabbing my coat off the rack, I double-checked that Byrd was nowhere near Benny, then skipped outside. The car took a few tries to start, which was completely understandable considering the drop in the temperature we'd experienced throughout the day. In truth, the cold weather had my brain feeling foggy and slow to start as well.

What was I thinking by getting involved in a case again? I had specifically told myself I would leave things alone and concentrate on what was important: the clinic. Yet here I was again, rushing across town to solve a puzzle as though the prize for winning was a lifetime supply of top-tier laboratory blood.

My phone rang, jerking me from my wandering

thoughts. Clicking the answer button so the call connected through Bluetooth, I slowed my speed and watched for patches of ice.

"Hi, Mom," I said.

"Lia! Finally," my mother screeched through the speakers. "Where have you been? I have called you a million times! I thought someone had staked you."

"You called once, Mom." I rolled my eyes at her dramatics. "And no one stakes vamps anymore. It's uncouth."

"Well, how was I supposed to know that when you literally abandoned me? Mothers can't help but worry!"

"I think that's a bit of an exaggeration," I said dryly. "Anyway, how's Dad doing?"

There was a guffaw on the other line, followed by a hoarse cough. My eyes darted to the phone. "Mom?"

"Yes, yes. Calm your britches," my mother said. "Your father is fine. We both got hit with a nasty cold, though. Must be this awful cold weather we're having."

I couldn't contain the laugh that poured out of me. My eyes watered as I continued to chuckle, turning off the main road and pulling into an empty parking place.

"You live in Florida, Mom. What cold weather?" I teased. "And vamps can't get sick. Please tell me you're not pretending to be ill for some absolutely unhinged reason."

"Don't be ridiculous. But if someone calls about discounted cough medication, just go with it, dear."

I grabbed my purse from the passenger seat and buttoned up my coat. Taking the phone off the stand, I tightened my jaw, knowing I needed to get off the call before I got roped into one of my mother's schemes again.

My teeth chattered as I pushed open the car door and stepped outside. Before me, Skeeter's bungalow hid behind a row of thick, lush pines, with only a sliver of the front porch showing.

Pressing the phone to my ear, I cut into my mom's rambling, "Listen, Mom, I'm really sorry, but I have to go. Tell Dad I said hi. I'll call you this weekend." Then, thinking about the last time she'd gotten one of her crazy ideas, I added, "And please don't do anything that will have you on the news before the holidays."

"Fine," my mom huffed out. "Are you dating someone yet?"

"Bye!" I screeched into the phone, hanging it up immediately.

With that looming disaster mostly out of the way, I set the phone on silent and tossed it into my purse. Making my way up the stone-lined path leading to the porch, I slowed to take in the scene. This was not the first time I'd visited Skeeter in his home, but each time, it made me pause.

It wasn't at all what one would imagine a troll's house would look like.

Twinkling Christmas lights were draped along the edges of the roofline like shimmering ice crystals; they were already on even though it wasn't dark yet. The house itself was painted a soft sage green, with a bright red door adorned by a wreath of deep green holly and pine cones. Two large bay windows, framed by white shutters, were on either side of the door, each dressed in frilly lace curtains. Through them I spotted a sparkling Christmas tree that was so tall, only someone Skeeter's height could reach the top. The bungalow's front porch had a pair of rocking chairs and a garland of pine wrapped along the railing they leaned against.

It was so cute I could barely handle it.

As I walked onto the porch, a flash of movement by the side of the house caught me off guard and I almost tripped over one of the rocking chairs. My hand jutted out quickly to break my fall seconds before my forehead collided with the wall. I steadied myself and looked to the right, where Skeeter's giant head was peering around the corner.

The troll's thick, bushy brows met in the center. "Lia?"

"Hey, Skeeter." I gave him a sheepish smile. "Sorry for the surprise visit. Do you have a couple of minutes? There's something I was hoping you could help me with."

"I was chopping some wood for the fire," the nearly seven-foot burly male replied, striding toward me. "But I sure could use a hot chocolate break. Come on in."

Skeeter was not a regular troll. Not by a long shot.

I followed the giant of a man through the front door, my muscles instantly relaxing once we were in the living room. If the outside of Skeeter's house was cute, the inside was like a fairy godmother's dream come true.

Cozy and welcoming, the living room was a patchwork of soft pastels and adorable details. A plush floral couch sat by the window beneath the lace curtains I'd spied from outside. Colorful quilts were draped over the armchairs, and a stone fireplace took up one corner. It was topped with shelves full of knick-knacks and old family photos.

Wooden beams ran across the ceiling, giving the space a rustic charm, while the smell of freshly baked cookies threw me completely off balance. It was like stepping into a story-book cottage.

I shook my head and grinned at the troll as he dumped another log into the fire. "Don't get me wrong, but I still can't believe this is your place."

"What's wrong with it?" Skeeter asked, his eyes rolling over the room questioningly.

"Nothing at all. It's perfect." I kicked off my boots and sighed. "And it's very cozy."

"Thanks," he said warmly. "Grennich helped pick out the paint colors. She has a great eye for design."

"Oh! That reminds me! Thank you for sending her my way. She has been an absolute blessing!"

"I figured you three would get along," the troll agreed. "Now about that hot chocolate…"

Chuckling, I shrugged off my coat and draped it on the wooden bench in the foyer. As I stepped deeper into the house, the warmth from the fireplace made every bone in my body relax, and I gravitated toward the couch like a moth to a flame. The moment I sat down, the cushions swallowed me whole.

"Vamp, remember?" I asked Skeeter. "Enjoy a mug for both of us."

He rapped his knuckles on his wide forehead. "Right.

Why don't you tell me what you need help with while I warm up a cup?"

The sweet smell of chocolate drifted from the small kitchen opposite the living room as Skeeter busied himself, creating the concoction he couldn't wait to drink. I sank further into the couch cushion while I filled the troll in on everything that had happened in the last few days.

I told him about each event in agonizing detail. Heck! It was as though I couldn't stop talking. There was no denying how nice it was to get it all off my chest. I could have told Bree about it, but after what happened with Justin, I didn't want to drag her into another dreadful mess. Not when she was spending so much time working at the clinic to help us get back into some semblance of normalcy.

But sitting there, talking to Skeeter, felt so natural. Normally, I poured all my energy into my career and it was easy to forget that having friends and a life were equally important. Maybe when things settled down, I could have everyone over for a nice holiday dinner. Ryder and Benny would love that, I was sure.

Why was I even thinking about Ryder at this moment?

I shook my head and kept on with the story. By the time I got to the part about seeing Dana's ex-husband acting dodgy at her apartment building, Skeeter was sitting on the armchair across from me with a gargantuan mug of hot chocolate in his hand. He lowered it onto the side table and pulled out his phone.

"What are you doing?" I asked.

"Looking for the ex." He lifted one eyebrow in question. "That's what you're here for, isn't it?"

"Well, yes, but don't you need some special computer or something?" I asked.

The troll didn't answer. His fingers typed rapidly, and creases lined his brow and the sides of his eyes as he pored over the phone, scrolling furiously.

Maybe Skeeter was underestimating how difficult this favor was. I tried again. "It's almost like the guy is a ghost. You might not even be able to find—"

He turned the screen around to face me. "This the guy?"

My jaw hit the floor. That was him. I was sure of it.

"How did you do that so fast? I couldn't find anything all day!"

"You only have to know where to look," Skeeter chuckled, his cheeks reddening. "His name is Lucas Jenkins. Lives on the opposite side of town, right near the falls. I'll text you the address."

I started to get up, but Skeeter was on his feet before me.

"On second thought," he said, downing his hot chocolate in one go. "Let me get my jacket. I'll come with you."

"You don't have to do that, Skeet!"

The troll waved me off. "'Course I do. Can't let you have all the fun, can I? You driving?"

I nodded and followed him to the door, the heat from the fireplace warming my retreating back. As I put on my coat and waited for Skeeter to get ready, only one thought flashed through my head. This giant man was going to be the guest of honor at my upcoming dinner. It seemed my mother had a point after all—life really was much better when you weren't all alone.

CHAPTER NINE

W hen it comes to ambushing a possible murder suspect, the key is to leave them no choice but to believe you are on their side. You have to make them feel safe, or at least that was what the university of true crime television and crime podcasts had taught me.

I repeated it like a mantra in my head, with Skeeter beside me, his ears twitching at every sudden noise. Together, we marched down Lucas Jenkins' street—a place that had seen far better days.

The buildings on either side rose high in the sky, their dirty walls blocking the sun and any warmth it might've cast down. The wind howled between the cracked alleyways, cutting through my jacket and rattling my bones with a cold that felt far more sinister than was necessary. I pulled my scarf tighter around my neck, but it did little to stop the icy chill that had seeped into my body.

As we passed by one dilapidated building, I noticed a window with torn blinds hanging at odd angles, barely concealing the broken glass beneath them. I grimaced, wondering how anyone could live like this. The entire neighborhood was a far cry from the posh area where Dana lived.

Overturned trashcans littered the sidewalks, their contents spilling out in nasty little heaps. The few town-houses that still stood were a patchwork of boarded-up windows and crumbling bricks, with long shadows stretching over the sidewalk like gangly fingers.

Aside from a couple of grumpy individuals who had bumped our shoulders several blocks back, the place felt completely abandoned. That was, if you didn't count the random shouts of anger that erupted from the building above us every now and then.

Despite the eerie quiet, I couldn't shake the feeling we were being watched. Every distant sound put my nerves on edge. Lucas lived here—if you could call it living—and if my hunch was right, he was tied to Dana's death somehow. Whether he'd speak to us or call the cops was anyone's guess, but the only way to find out was to keep moving forward.

I glanced over my shoulder, then sped up, eager to get this over with so we could leave.

"You said the wife lived on Baker Street?" Skeeter asked.

I nodded, my pace continuing to grow quicker. "Uh-huh. Are you thinking what I'm thinking?"

"If this guy had anything to do with what happened to her, it was probably money related."

"Sadly, people have killed for less," I said. "But for all we know, Dana died of natural causes, like the police assume. So let's not go in there with all our 'guns' blazing."

Skeeter smiled. "How about just our safety off?"

"Sounds like a plan."

We walked another block before I noticed the rusty metal number nailed to one building and checked my phone. "This is it."

Exchanging looks of trepidation, we pried open the creaking front door of the apartment building and made our way into what was supposed to be a lobby, if you could have even called it that. The dank space we entered was a mirror of the outside with ageing wallpaper peeling away from water-stained walls and the stench of something I refused to pinpoint.

I pulled up my scarf over my nose, motioning toward the staircase off to the left. "It doesn't look like there's an elevator."

Skeeter snorted. "I'm surprised there's a staircase."

We headed up the stairs, climbing the first few floors fairly quickly. It's shocking how fast one is willing to move when they can't wait to get out of a place. When we reached the third floor, I checked left and right, following the rising numbers to the end of a decrepit hallway.

The solid wood door of unit 312 was painted a sickly

shade of pea-soup green and there was a rusty knocker in the shape of a lion's head nailed below the peephole. I squared my shoulders and gave it a good tap. After waiting a few moments without a response, I reached out and tried the knocker again.

"Maybe he's not home," Skeeter whispered.

As soon as the words tumbled from his lips, the door swung open and the man I'd seen at the park poked his head through the opening. My chest tightened, and I fought the urge to leap backward to hide behind Skeeter.

"Who are you?" Lucas asked gruffly. His sneer deflated the instant he noticed Skeeter's towering shape behind me. "Are you two selling something? Unless it's girl club cookies, I don't want any of it."

"Not at all, Mr. Jenkins," I said, forcing a weak smile. "My name is Ophelia Pane, and this is my friend, Skeeter Kraus. We were hoping to ask you a few questions about your ex-wife."

Lucas's eyebrows shot up into his receding hairline. The movement was so quick it would have been comical—if not for the attitude that followed. He straightened his spine, adding an inch to his too-thin frame, as if preparing for battle. His nostrils flared, and his angry glare was icy enough to make the air feel instantly colder.

For a moment, I saw something dark surface and swirl in his eyes, but he quickly pushed it back. It would've been terrifying if I hadn't known that I could drop the man on his butt in seconds and Skeeter would likely do much worse if the human tried anything.

I wasn't afraid, but one thing was quite clear from the man's stance: Lucas Jenkins did not want to talk about Dana. Not now. Not ever. The very mention of her name had struck a nerve too deep.

I wondered if the anger I'd seen in him had been strong enough to act on. To kill over, perhaps.

"I don't have anything to say about Dana," he bit out. "If you're sniffing around looking for gossip for a story, I'll tell you the same thing I told the other clowns. My ex-wife was a lot to handle, but the world is a worse place without her in it."

My lips parted, letting out a sharp breath. "There were reporters here?"

"Are you kidding? I haven't been able to cross the street without them hounding me ever since the police came around." He studied Skeeter. "Though you don't look like a reporter to me."

Skeeter shrugged. "That's because we're not."

Lucas leaned against the doorjamb. "Then why are you here? How did you know Dana?"

"She was training my dog," I lied.

"Ah. Well, why didn't you say that in the first place?" The sudden change in his expression was nerve-wracking. The man went from a raging bull to Mr. Sunshine in seconds. His lips curved into what he probably thought was a welcoming smile. "What did you need with me?"

I shot a sideway glance up at Skeeter, clearing my throat. "First, I'd like to offer my condolences. I hadn't realized Dana was married."

"Not anymore," Lucas corrected. "But we were working it out."

Were you now?

"Right, of course. You know, now that I think of it, you look fairly familiar," I added, tilting my head as though trying to place him. "I think I saw you with Dana at the dog park a few days back."

There was a flash of panic behind Lucas's eyes, but he corrected himself quickly. "Did you?" He scratched his neck, the skin under his five o'clock shadow reddening. "I don't remember meeting you."

"I didn't introduce myself that day," I said. "You two seemed to be in a bit of a spat, so I didn't want to interrupt."

Lucas swallowed hard. "You'll have to be more specific." To my utter surprise, he barked a laugh. "As I'm sure you know, Dana was a passionate woman. There were few conversations that didn't turn into arguments with her."

"Must have been hard on the marriage," Skeeter said. "Dealing with that."

"Are you kidding? It was the best part."

Had I heard him correctly?

He grinned. "Look, I'm not going to explain my marriage to two strangers, but let's say that the more heated the arguments, the better the make-up was."

All right, I did not need that explanation. I clenched my teeth together to keep the nausea at bay. Doing my best to keep a smile plastered on my face, I inched closer to Skeeter, my boot knocking against his. The troll looked down at me in solidarity.

"Th… That's good," I stammered, unsure how to respond.

"It really was."

Ew. Please stop. Struggling against the urge to hightail it back down the stairs, I said, "Mr. Jenkins, can I ask you a serious question?" When Lucas nodded, I continued, "Do you think your ex-wife died accidentally?"

"Well, what else would it be?" Lucas asked, baffled. "Although…"

He stopped speaking, his mouth snapping closed like it had been zippered shut. The silence stretched between us until I found my skin starting to itch at the awkwardness.

What was going on? What was he not telling us?

Lucas sighed and rubbed his eyes. "Look, I don't even know why I'm telling you this, but…"

I leaned in closer. "But?"

"Dana had this neighbor who always rubbed me the wrong way. She moved into that place of hers without doing any research on the other people living there," Lucas explained. "I told her a million times that neighborhoods like that come with trouble, but she didn't listen. Dana told me her business was finally taking off, and come Hades or high water, she was going to enjoy the fruits of her labor."

Glancing around the hallway, I decided I couldn't blame the woman for wanting to escape the treacherous dump.

"Anyway, this guy was constantly hounding her about

bringing the dogs she trained home. A real grouch, you know the type." Lucas lifted his hands in mock surrender. "I'm not saying he did something, of course. It was an accident, no question about it. But you asked if I could think of someone, and he's the first one that came to mind. Don't think anything of it."

I was saved from responding when my phone beeped. "I thought I put this on silent! I'm terribly sorry." Wincing, I reached into my bag to turn it off. When I did, my stomach seized at the name flashing on the screen.

Leaving Skeeter to finish up with the ex-husband, I excused myself and stepped further down the hallway. Sweat trickled down my neck as I put some distance between me and the men before I opened the unread text message.

Clicking on the bubble, I read it in my head, then once more in a whisper under my breath. Ryder's name at the top of the screen made my head spin, but it was what he wrote that had the biggest effect on me.

I read the message a third time, my stomach twisting itself in knots. "You have got to be kidding me."

CHAPTER TEN

"What are you talking about? I've never heard of a supernatural wanted list!" I hissed into the phone. This was a weird joke, right?

A throat cleared on the other end of the line as Ryder collected himself. Like he hadn't listened to me absolutely freak out for the last five minutes of our call.

"Some supernaturals are not meant to mingle with humans," he explained. "The Supe Justice Department handles such cases by isolating dangerous magical creatures before their full powers come into effect and endanger the public. It is a necessary precaution to keep paranormals hidden and out of danger."

When I didn't say anything, he sighed heavily. "I thought everyone in the supernatural community knew about this."

"Well, clearly not everyone," I whispered between clenched teeth.

Did my parents know about the Supe Justice Department? If so, why had they kept it from me? I was going to be so mad if that was the case.

Settling my rising nerves, I paced the length of the alley behind Lucas's apartment building while Skeeter waited by the car. "And you're saying Benny is on the list?"

Ryder sighed again. "Afraid so. Someone spotted him at the dog park."

"How did they even know he wasn't a regular puppy?"

"I have no idea," he said. "But try to stay out of sight for now. I'll think of something when I get back. How's he doing, anyhow?"

I rolled my eyes. "Oh, he's great. Having the time of his life."

"And you?"

"Good as I can be." I pinched the bridge of my nose. "We hired a new vet, so that's been great. Listen, Ryder. I have to go," I told the detective. "I'll make sure to keep Benny inside and will only walk him at night. And I might have an idea for how to keep him out of trouble. Let me look into it and we'll talk more when you're back in town."

"Sure thing," Ryder said. "And Lia? Don't do anything dangerous if you can help it."

"No promises," I said, hanging up before he could question me further.

The walk to the car to meet Skeeter felt longer than the actual forty-five seconds it had taken to get there. I couldn't believe what was happening. Since when was there a special department of supernaturals, and why did they care about Benny?

I mean, sure, a hellhound on earth didn't sound great, but Benny was a sweet little baby who couldn't harm a fly. The memory of him chasing Byrd around flashed before my eyes. That was different, though—the bat had probably instigated the trouble.

Climbing into the car, I closed the door a lot harder than I'd intended to.

"Everything all right?" Skeeter asked, one brow rising.

On any other day, I'd have laughed at his giant figure folded into the passenger seat. Today, however, I had no sense of humor left.

I rolled down the window to let the cold air blast at my face. "Did you know there's a supernatural task force? Like a government of some sort?"

"The SJD? Of course," the troll said. "I work for them from time to time. Why?"

"No reason," I grumbled. "Did the ex say anything else in there after I left?"

"Nothing important. But I had the chance to do some digging on the neighbor he mentioned while you were on the phone."

Well, consider my interest piqued and my good mood restored. I tucked away the recent development on the hellhound front and focused on Skeeter. There would be plenty of time to worry about the dog situation later. As long as I kept

Benny out of sight, he would be fine until we found a more permanent solution.

It was something I hoped Grennich could help with, but I wouldn't know more until I had the chance to speak to her. And the plan would require me to reveal the truth about Benny to her, which I still wasn't sure about.

For now, though, there were more urgent matters to handle.

Turning to face Skeeter, I rested my arm on the steering wheel and asked, "What did you find?"

"You're not going to believe this." The troll tapped on his phone and showed me the screen.

As I read, my jaw gaped until it nearly rested squarely on my thighs. Was this what I thought it was? It seemed outrageous, but people did bizarre things when they were upset. And it appeared Buster Albright was no exception to that rule.

The man had created an entire website dedicated to the people in the building he felt violated their community standards. He was even documenting some of them with pictures. I wondered how much of it was legal and made a mental note to ask Ryder about it later. From my perspective, the nosy neighbor should have been slapped with a ticket of some kind. At what point did someone cross the line and go from being a concerned neighbor to being a stalker or a peeping Tom? At the very least, Buster Albright needed a stern talking to from the police.

Hmm. I wonder if the cops know about this?

I quickly read the rest of the website, then looked at

Skeeter. "Can you send that to me? I have some time before my shift tonight and want to see what else I can dig up on this website."

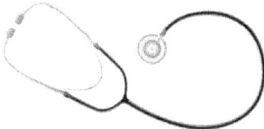

TWO HOURS LATER, I was three boxes of Crimson Quench and five pages of handwritten notes deep in my research. I sat at the kitchen island with Benny nestled at my feet and Byrd curled up in the empty fruit basket. Several tabs from Buster's terrifying stalker website were open on my laptop, and I switched between them as I continued furiously scribbling down notes.

The man was so meticulously detailed; it was a surprise he had time to sleep. Between the elderly woman on the first floor who had one too many cats, the guy in the penthouse who played his music a decibel too loud after eight at night, and the family on the fifth floor with rowdy children, it seemed like Buster Albright had his hands full reporting on every infraction committed by his neighbors.

Not even the poor mailman had escaped inclusion on the unhinged complaint site. Buster had dedicated an entire page to complaining about the envelopes not being perfectly lined up in the mailboxes. It was so bizarre that it was almost comical.

Though I doubted his neighbors felt the same way.

I slid off the barstool to pet Benny behind the ears. "Can you believe this guy, Benny?"

The dog cocked his head, opened his mouth in a wide yawn, and let his tongue loll out the side as he settled back down.

I chuckled. "My thoughts exactly."

Snatching another blood box from the fridge, I carried the laptop and notebook to my bedroom so I could keep perusing it while I got ready for work. As I brushed out the mess my red waves had become, a post from a month ago caught my attention.

I dropped the comb on the bed and leaned in closer to the screen. "Interesting."

It seemed Buster had enough of a problem with Dana that he'd started a petition to get her dog training business closed. According to the blog post, he had spoken to her several times, and she'd refused to stop bringing her clients into the building for training.

Buster held the opinion that having those dogs on the building's grounds would affect anyone with allergies— which would have been a fair point had the building not been pet friendly.

Case and point: the woman on the first floor with five cats.

So why had this man been so fixated on Dana? Or did he just hate dogs?

I clicked on the live spreadsheet linked in the post, my eyes rounding. By some miracle, Buster had managed to gather almost a dozen signatures from fellow neighbors.

Were there other people in the building who'd wanted Dana gone too?

I jotted another note on the page: *Check the petition names.*

Completely abandoning my attempt to get ready, I opened a new tab and ran a search for Buster's name, this time including Dana's as well. There were a few hits, but one article from a year ago stood out from the rest. When I clicked it, the reason for Buster's animosity toward her became abundantly clear.

"No way," I whispered into the emptiness of my bedroom.

Dana had tried to have Buster evicted almost one year to the date when she'd found out about his neighborhood watch website. According to the article, the entire fiasco had made it far enough to attract the attention of the local news, and the police had become involved when Buster threatened the dog trainer.

No wonder he wanted revenge.

I continued to check the rest of the search results, but nothing yielded much more information. A few pages down, another blog popped up with Buster's name attached to it. Clicking it took me to a website that was primarily photos of the man at different events around the town.

In the pictures, he didn't match the vision of him I'd created in my head. He had medium length brown hair that was expertly styled in a side part. The thick-framed glasses he wore had all the fashion of a modern day creative and his clothing was straight off a runway. If I'd seen these photos before, I never would have pegged the man to be a neighborhood grouch.

In some pictures, Buster actually looked quite happy.

My gaze zeroed in on one photo of him smiling widely with a theater sign behind him. I instantly recognized the name of the musical, having tried to get tickets for it, but unfortunately, they'd been sold out for months, what with there only being one showing. Buster, however, had managed to snag a ticket without a problem.

A new realization hit me right as Benny trotted into the room, and I looked down at the pup with a grimace.

"There goes that lead, buddy," I sighed.

There was no way Buster could have done anything to Dana. The musical had played on the same evening as Dana had been found in the park, and it was all the way in Halston Hills, a four-hour drive from our town.

Buster Albright may have hated the dog trainer, but he hadn't wanted to hurt her. Which meant I was back at square one.

Great.

CHAPTER ELEVEN

I took the side streets to get to the clinic when it came time to open for the evening shift. With Benny on some mysterious watchlist for the even more mysterious SJD, I wasn't willing to take the risk of someone seeing him. And a woman trotting down the street with a hellhound on a leash and a bat in a carrier would surely draw some attention.

My stomach tensed as I approached the turn toward the more open area of the street. Fingers and toes crossed, I darted past a few people dotting the sidewalk and practically threw myself and the animals into the clinic, closing the door behind us with a definitive click.

The darkness of the waiting room enveloped me. It was so dense that I couldn't see an inch in front of my face. Benny hid between my legs, his tail tucked in.

"Let me turn the light on, buddy," I said. "There's nothing to be afraid of in here."

I placed Byrd's carrier on a chair and felt the wall for the switch. As soon as the light came on, I shrieked. There were two figures standing in the middle of the waiting room, staring right at me.

"Bree! Grennich!" I screamed, clutching at my chest. "What are you two doing standing around in the dark? You nearly gave me a heart attack!"

"See? Told you vamps are really jumpy," Bree stated matter-of-factly, as though that explained anything.

"Huh. You're right," Grennich replied. "I had no idea! Coffee's on me next time."

I removed my trembling hand and took the leash off Benny, letting the pup run off into the depth of the clinic and away from the unhinged duo cackling in front of me.

"Did you place a bet on whether or not you could scare me by just standing there?" I asked, still working to slow my breathing.

"Obviously," Bree snickered. "And I won fair and square!"

I shook my head, my eyes rolling skyward. "You will be the death of me."

"Unlikely!" Bree snorted. "Vamps are notoriously hard to kill."

"Well, death by jumpscare might get added to the list if you two keep this up." Biting my bottom lip, I took off my coat and made sure the front door was locked before beckoning them both further into the clinic.

When we reached one of the exam rooms, I ushered the techs inside, then I slid out of the room to find Benny. While I was out, I made sure to take my time, letting Byrd out of the carrier and checking on today's patient schedule. By the time I returned, both Grennich and Bree had their arms crossed and their jaws tense with anticipation.

Good. Teaches them right for playing tricks on me.

"So why'd you call us in early?" Bree asked, shifting her weight from one foot to the other.

I gave the pup a doggy treat and sat him down on the examination table, settling in beside him. "I need your help. It's a sensitive topic, so I'll need you both to keep an open mind when I tell you the problem."

Waiting for them to nod in agreement, I fed Benny another treat, then told the techs everything. After another call with Ryder, I'd finally convinced him that Bree and Grennich could be trusted with Benny's secret. Now I was eager to see what ideas they could come up with.

A healing fae and a pixie were not to be trifled with when it came to their abilities with magic, and I knew between the three of us we could come up with a plan to keep the dog safe—or at least a temporary solution until Ryder returned, so I didn't have to sneak around alleyways with the hellhound every day.

As I spoke, I expected to hear gasps of shock and to be bombarded with a million questions. Instead, the pair stayed cool and collected. In truth, I shouldn't have been surprised. We dealt with far more surprising things at the clinic on a near weekly basis.

When I got to the part about the SJD, I paused. Neither Bree nor Grennich batted an eyelash at the mention of the organization.

"Am I the only one who didn't know about this part of the paranormal world?" I asked, throwing up my hands.

"Kinda seems like it." Bree looked like she was trying not to laugh. "It's pretty common knowledge. Or at least it is among the paranormals in Bluejay Falls. Maybe it's because you aren't a local?"

"But I'm not from here either and I've heard about it." Grennich pointed out.

"Or maybe you were sheltered and need to start getting out of your coffin more?" Bree teased, trying but failing to hide her grin this time.

"Yeah, yeah. Whatever," I huffed.

She was probably right, and it likely had something to do with the way my overprotective mother kept me from asking too many questions.

"So, what do you think? Does Benny have any shot of outsmarting the SJD, or are we in trouble?" I asked, wanting to focus back on the issue at hand.

"I'm not sure," Bree said at the same time as Grennich yelled out, "I have an idea!"

The pixie and I swung our heads toward her in unison. I cradled Benny closer to my chest, unable to control the excitement bubbling up in my chest. *I knew it was a good plan to ask them!*

Breath speeding up, I focused my attention on the fae. "What are you thinking?"

"When I was little, I used to hate playing hide and seek." The fae tapped her chin. "I come from a large family and I was always the smallest of the group, and the worst one at hiding."

"I'm not sure I follow," I said, scratching behind the hellhound's ear. "What does this have to do with Benny?"

Grennich held up a finger before continuing to explain. "The day I turned thirteen and was old enough to take up real magic, do you know what the first spell I learned was?"

"Recovery?" Bree guessed.

The fae clicked her tongue. "Nope! I tried my hand at a magic cloaking spell—a way to prevent others from sensing my magic near them. See, I didn't care about finding the others," she said. "All I wanted was some peace and quiet and to be left out of their games. Eight siblings, you know? I figured if I could cloak myself from their prying eyes, they'd leave me alone."

"Did they?"

"For a while," she said. "Then I got bored and started playing, anyway. But the point is, I can use the same spell on Benny and cloak him from anyone with the ability to sense magic."

"Grennich! You're a genius!" I yelped. "Do you really think that could work?"

"Only one way to find out." The fae wiggled her brows mischievously.

Twenty minutes later, the clinic examination room had been given a complete makeover. My eyes widened in surprise, unable to recognize the clinical space the room had been a short while before.

Grennich had set up an entire operation from things she'd found around the office and items she already had in her bag of tricks—an arsenal for "just in case" situations, as she called them. She'd moved everything out of the way to make a large empty space in the center, and she'd lined the walls with lit candles.

Our kettle was filled with herbs and potions she'd pulled from her traveling stash. She finished by turning down the lights and putting on a classical music playlist to help her concentrate.

If I didn't know this was a vet clinic, I'd have thought I was in a healer's lab, or some type of weird yoga retreat massage room. It was pretty amazing.

I slowly gathered my jaw off the floor. "Grennich, you're kind of amazing."

"Ha! How about you wait to see if my plan works before saying that?"

She motioned for us to put Benny in the center of the circle and to step aside. I didn't like leaving the little guy, but he seemed much too interested in the crystals Grennich laid out to care about being magically experimented on.

As she began her work, my stomach twisted itself into a pretzel of anxiety and my mind raced. What if something went wrong?

No, I had to trust in Grennich. She was more than capable with magic. Not to mention that we didn't exactly have many other ideas to keep Benny safe and away from the SJD.

When Ryder had told me about the department, he hadn't been clear on what exactly would happen to Benny if he were caught, but I got the sense that it wasn't anything good.

This had to work.

Soft fingers looped over mine. I turned my head toward Bree as she gave my hand a squeeze.

"He'll be fine," she whispered.

I smiled, my lips tight and tense.

Crouching before us, Grennich continued her low whispering chants while Benny pawed at the crystals. Her words jumbled together, the speed of the sentences rising with the pitch of her voice.

Smoke burst from the kettle, swirling around her and Benny. I watched in amazement as her eyes snapped open to reveal bright white orbs that lit up the entire room. With her arms stretch out, she placed her hands on either side of Benny's face.

The red flames on each candle turned a bright neon green. I gasped as Benny's small body glowed a similar shade and he floated a foot off the floor.

My throat tightened. "Is that supposed to happen?"

Behind me, the door to the exam room burst open as Byrd crashed inside. The bat shot past Bree and me, flying into the center of the smoke and candles... and straight toward Benny.

I screamed. Bree laughed. Grennich lost her focus on the magic.

With the spell disrupted, I assumed the dog would float back down, but that didn't happen. Instead, he seemed to rise higher, and Byrd was all the more excited to chase after him. When they reached the ceiling, they tumbled around, playfully scrapping as they raced across the ceiling tiles.

"Let me guess." I side-glanced at Grennich, who avoided looking in my direction. "He's not cloaked?"

"Definitely not," the fae answered, crossing her arms over her chest and shaking her head in disbelief. "I think his hellhound magic interfered with mine. I've worked this spell many times before and this is the first time anyone floated."

"What about the glow?" Bree asked.

"Yeah, that's new too," Grennich muttered.

Bree chuckled. "Looks like you have competition for the king of the skies, Byrd!"

The three of us stood in stunned silence as the bat and the dog continued their game of ceiling chase. Well, there went that plan.

I watched Byrd fly at Benny. The dog swerved out of the way, his green glowing body bouncing off the wall and floating back toward the bat. I knew we had to get Benny back down at some point, but I couldn't bring myself to interrupt their good time yet.

Bree's comment replayed in my head. A bat and a dog competing in flight were not something I thought I'd witness in my lifetime.

Hmm, I thought, watching them play. Competition…

Despite our failure with Benny, a smile spread across my face. The pixie didn't know it, but she'd given me a good idea—one that could help me figure out what had happened to Dana once and for all.

CHAPTER
TWELVE

Standing in front of Pawsitive Academy, all I felt was shock. Who knew that dog training businesses were so lucrative? I certainly hadn't.

While Dana ran her dog training services out of the comfort of her home, her competitor was an exact opposite.

The academy was set back from the main road—a long path carved out between two forested areas—with a gravel driveway winding past an abandoned well painted a bright red. The sign at the entrance—a hand-painted board hanging by chains from a wooden arch—read *Pawsitive Academy: Training with Heart*. That should have been my first clue that this place would be as bizarre as it was pretentious.

As I drove toward the main entrance, an oversized log cabin came into view, with a weathered red tin roof that gleamed in the sun. Several large flower boxes lined the porch, and wind chimes tinkled in the breeze. I listened for the sound of dogs barking, but the place was so quiet that it bordered on the uncomfortable.

I pulled into a parking place in front of the cabin. Climbing out of my car, I noticed a sign pointing visitors around the back of the main building and I followed the bone-shaped arrow. As I skirted around the side of the building, I caught sight of an agility course, where a petite young blonde held up a loop. A tiny terrier slightly larger than Benny hopped through the circle with ease, its ears pricked and tail wagging.

Is it weird I'm here without a dog?

I instantly regretted not bringing Benny along, although that would have been impossible, thanks to him being lit up like a glow stick.

Pulling beyond the agility course, a grass-covered field stretched toward a dense tree line. There was another sign, but this one had the words *Meditation Walk* carved into it. There was no stopping my involuntary eye roll.

Turning back toward the cabin, I spotted another door on the backside, and one that appeared to have seen heavy use. I gave the blonde playing with the dog another glance, then pushed the door open and walked inside.

My boots squeaked against the polished wood floor as I entered the reception area. It was quieter than I'd expected, but I could hear soft music playing from somewhere nearby. Shelves lined the waiting area, each with an assortment of magazines about pet wellness, animal psychology, and holistic health. It was an interesting combination.

A hallway led deeper into the cabin. Its walls were decorated with various flyers and brochures that advertised all sorts of upcoming community events and rallies for homeless pets in need.

Striding to the main desk, I studied the photo board on the wall behind it. The board depicted images of dogs, each pinned with a paw-shaped sticker marking their "graduation" from the academy.

The place was cute, and they took obvious pride in paying attention to details, but even as someone who worked with dogs on a near-daily basis, it was a bit over the top for my liking. I got the distinct impression they were more focused on catering to the owners' egos, rather than the needs of the dogs they were training.

Yeah, Benny was so not coming here. As soon as the thought crossed my mind, I reminded myself that the hellhound was not my dog. Although I doubted Ryder would disagree with my assessment of this place.

"Welcome to Pawsitive Academy!"

I jumped, startled.

Huh! Maybe Bree is right about vampires being easy to scare...

Spinning on my heels, I followed the sound of the high-pitched voice. My eyes focused on the woman who had stepped up behind me.

Her pale hair was pulled back in a ponytail that was so

high it seemed to be erupting from the top of her head like a blonde geyser. The woman's gray eyes traveled over me and her smile tightened as though she were trying to keep it from slipping off her face.

Her false cheerfulness made me dislike her immediately. She reminded me of the people who sprayed perfume on you at the mall, whether you asked them to or not. A little too happy and pushy.

Telling myself that I shouldn't judge someone within moments of meeting them, I returned her smile and cleared my throat. "Thanks so much. Great place you have here."

"We try our best. Are you here to enquire about dog training services?" the woman asked. "As you may have guessed, we have a more holistic approach to dog training, unlike some other places, and we take great pride in all our furry heroes. Were you looking for full-time placement, or are you interested in one of our doggy meditation packages?"

I'm sorry, what? Did she say "doggy meditation?"

I'd believed the meditation aspects of the business were directed at humans. The idea of Benny, or any dog, sitting in silence, was so laughable that I stiffened my shoulders to keep them from shaking at the thought.

This place was even more bizarre than I'd originally assumed. But it also appeared to be well liked considering all the photos on the wall. Perhaps I needed to give it another shot before judging.

"Our monthly puppy poetry session is starting in an hour. You're welcome to sit in to test it out."

Nevermind. I hadn't been exaggerating.

This place was completely unhinged. Most puppies still needed to learn what the word potty meant, let alone practicing poetry. I quickly scanned the room, wondering if I was being pranked, but it seemed she was serious.

My lips trembled as I tried not to laugh in the woman's face. "Um, I was actually hoping to speak to the owner, Karen Wells?"

"Ah, well, why didn't you say so?" the woman exclaimed, patting her hair. "You got her right here."

Oh, sweet dairy.

I held out my hand. "It's wonderful to meet you, Karen. My name is Ophelia Pane."

"Do you have a dog in need of training, Miss Pane?" Karen shook my offered hand, then rubbed her palm against her jeans as though afraid I'd gotten her dirty.

How did this woman work with dogs?

"Not exactly. I'm a veterinarian and own Sunny Days Animal Clinic." When she didn't immediately respond, I decided to plunge ahead. "Did you know a woman by the name of Dana Seller? She was also a dog trainer."

Karen's smile was replaced by a stern frown. "I'm afraid I can't help you."

She shifted uncomfortably, her gaze darting to the side as if weighing the consequences of what she might say.

"But I didn't say what I needed yet…"

"That's enough." Karen's tone was low and clipped, the kind that could shut down even the most persistent of interrogations.

It was clear she had no intention of divulging any details or gossip about the death of her rival. She widened her stance as if to tell me she meant business and that I shouldn't try to cross her. When she folded her arms over her chest, I knew I was about to be kicked to the curb.

"Look," Karen said, her voice softening a fraction. "I heard about what happened to Dana, and I'm sorry. But she was not a good person. And she was not a good trainer. I don't want to speak ill of the dead, so it is best you leave."

Pasting on my friendliest smile, I tried again. "I promise not to take more than another minute or two of your time. Just one more question—"

Karen cut me off. "You should go. Thank you for coming by." Her lips tightened into a line so thin I could no longer see them. "If any of your patients need a trainer who actually cares for their dogs, send them our way."

With that, she twirled around and marched past the counter and into a darkened hallway that took her deeper into the cabin and away from me. Her steps echoed for a few seconds, then vanished entirely, leaving me alone in the reception area.

I huffed out an exasperated breath. The smell of patchouli filled my nose, and I instantly stifled a sneeze. Honestly, I should've gotten out of here sooner. The academy was way too over the top. Besides, what dog enjoyed incense, unless it came in the scent of fresh cat poop, butcher shop bones, or expensive leather shoes?

I started for the door, but before I could reach for the handle, it swung open. The same young woman I'd spotted working outside marched into the room, her brow slick with sweat.

She regarded me with a questioning glare, as though I'd offended her simply by existing. "Has someone been by to help you?"

I shrugged.

"Oh, well, name's Casey," the girl said. "My aunt runs this place. I can go get her for you if you like."

"I don't think that will be necessary," I admitted. "I'm not here for training services. In fact, I was hoping to ask your aunt something about a competitor of hers, but she wasn't in the mood to chat."

The girl's forehead creased. "Are you talking about Dana Seller?"

I nodded slowly.

"Well, no wonder! Aunt Karen and her did not get along. At all."

"Yes, I gathered as much," I breathed out.

Casey approached me tentatively, dropping a leash into a basket on the floor that was filled with others in every hue imaginable. She picked up a clipboard from a nearby table and checked something off. Placing the board back on the table, she faced me head on.

"Maybe I can help," she offered.

"Really? That would be amazing," I said excitedly. "Did you know Dana well?"

"I didn't know her at all."

My hope deflated like a popped balloon. "I see. Any chance you might know if your aunt and Dana had any disagreements other than competing for the same business?"

Her eyes narrowed and her jaw set.

"I'm not suggesting anything," I quickly corrected. "I know Dana had a… a strong personality."

"Ha! That's putting it mildly. The woman was obnoxious and rude." Casey walked past me to the counter, opening up a laptop. The light from it illuminated her tanned skin, making her seem even younger. "But if you're hoping to find someone who had beef with her, you should talk to Sara."

I took a small step forward, closing in on her. "Who's that?"

"Sara Cline," the girl replied. "She's one of our new clients, but she used to be Dana's. From what I heard, there was some major drama between them. She is definitely not a fan."

"She left Dana on bad terms?"

"You can say that again," Casey snorted. "Last I heard, she was suing Dana. I don't know why, though."

Before I could ask her to elaborate, Karen's sharp voice shouted from somewhere inside the cabin. "Casey! Time to get ready for the poetry session!"

The young girl cringed visibly. She closed the lid of the laptop with a slam, gathering a stack of papers from the counter and tucking them under her arm.

With a sheepish smile, she stepped around me, jerking her chin in the direction Karen's voice had come from. "I should probably go. Those puppies get wild if they don't get their fix of Emily Dickinson."

She was gone before I could tell her that the puppies wouldn't know Dickinson from Dr. Seuss.

As I stood there in the middle of an empty reception area that reeked of incense that assaulted my senses, my heart jolted in my chest. The long drive over here hadn't been a bust after all. I had a lead—a proper lead! Whoever this ex-client was, I needed to speak with her.

My eyes landed on the laptop. Now if I could only find out where the woman lived…

Ignoring the sense of guilt that immediately began gnawing at my insides, I leaped behind the counter and opened the laptop, praying the academy didn't believe in password protection.

Luckily for me, they didn't.

Keeping one eye on the hallway, I checked the files, finding the client list fairly quickly. I scrolled through the names. And scrolled. And scrolled.

Geez. This place sure was popular.

"Bingo!" I whisper-cheered when I saw Sara Cline's name listed.

Using a Post-It note I found on the counter, I jotted down the address, closed the laptop, and darted out the door. My pulse raced the entire time I speed-walked back to the car, and I all but dove into the driver's seat when I reached it. Foot on the gas pedal, I sped away from Pawsitive Academy, leaving the log cabin in the dust.

The last thing I needed was for Karen to catch on to

what I'd done and punish me by forcing me to listen to her read poetry to dogs. I was finding it hard to believe people willingly paid good money to take part in that.

Checking the clock on the dash, I picked up speed and turned the car toward town. I had just enough time to make a quick stop before work.

Fingers crossed, Sara Cline would be more welcoming.

CHAPTER THIRTEEN

I

t turned out Sara Cline was not welcoming at all.

When I reached the address listed in the Pawsitive Academy's client records, I was in awe of the stunning mid-century home on one of the more exclusive residential streets.

I tried my best to appear non-threatening when walking toward her front door. After all, I was bombarding the woman in her home. Not to mention, I'd done some creepy stalker-ish crap to get her address.

And in her defense, I could be pushy when my mind was set on something.

Thanks for that trait, Mom.

But all of that still did not excuse how the woman flung open her door and threatened to call the cops within seconds of seeing me approach. It didn't help that her dog continued to bark incessantly even after I'd convinced Sara that I meant no harm.

Then there was the incident of me tripping over what was apparently her pride and joy: a pile of random stones stacked in an odd shape in her driveway. It turned out the stones were an abstract sculpture Sara had been working on for weeks to get just right. It looked like the landscapers had just tossed them there, but I never had understood abstract art.

To put it short, my plan to get information out of her was not off to a great start.

I stood a good four feet from the rocks in question, with Sara glaring at me tightlipped from the top step of the front porch. Her foot tapped out a pattern on the wooden planks, likely eager to get me out of her hair.

"Again, I'm really sorry to barge in on you like this," I said meekly.

Sara's blue eyes narrowed to near slits. "You said you're a vet?" When I nodded my agreement, she asked, "Why are you here? Roxie is in pristine health."

I glanced toward the large bay window where Roxie lounged in what looked like a diamond encrusted doggie bed. The poodle watched me with disdain, making me do a double take at how much she looked like her owner.

Am I really so hard to trust? I shook my head to clear that thought.

My patients loved me, and I would not let one dog and her overly cautious owner undermine my self-esteem.

Not today, Roxie!

"Actually," I said, sticking to the story I'd come up with on the way over here. "I am looking to recommend a dog training school to some of my patients, and was wondering if you could let me know about your experience with Pawsitive Academy."

The ice behind Sara's eyes melted, and her shoulders relaxed. She glanced at the poodle in the window, giving her two thumbs up. At that, the dog seemed to relax as well, and for a second, I could have sworn I saw Roxie smirk.

I tried to hide my relief that my cover story had earned me some trust from both of them.

Across from me, Sara beamed, all her previous annoyance gone. "Why didn't you say so?" she asked with a giggle.

Because you were one step away from getting a shotgun.

I grimaced, then quickly wiped the expression from my face. "So, the academy. How has your experience been there?"

"Roxie absolutely adores it! She is like a new dog since we started going there. And the poetry sessions have had a tremendous effect on her creativity. Truly, I couldn't say enough good things about the place," Sara cooed.

"And they've done wonderful things for the rescues as well." She raked her fingers through her glossy brown waves, the gargantuan diamond on her finger ripping a few strands out, although Sara didn't appear to notice. "Your patients will love it there! They might get put on a waiting list for some services because of space limitations. It can get cramped if all her clients show up, but I assure you the wait is well worth it!"

I forced a smile. "That's great to hear. You said you noticed a visible change in Roxie since starting there?"

"Most definitely. She is much more calm now."

I looked in the window where Roxie was running in circles, the doggie bed abandoned and kicked to the side. She bounded off the leather couch and jumped in the air. Her paws hit the window, where she used her speed to perform a perfect backflip. The second she landed, she was back to running circles.

Oh, yeah. Her calmness was truly overwhelming.

I pulled my gaze away from the circus going on inside the house and concentrated on Sara. "I'm glad you two had such a wonderful experience there. It was between Pawsitive Academy and another trainer, a Dana Seller, and I was hoping to get some referrals for both before deciding on the one the clinic will endorse."

At the mere mention of Dana's name, Sara's entire demeanor shifted, as if someone had flipped a switch. Her posture went stiff and stoney, like she was squaring up for a fight.

Sara's face darkened, casting shadows over her features, and her lips curled into a vicious sneer. Her eyes narrowed into a hard, frigid glare that could have cut glass and her hands clenched into white-knuckled fists at her sides.

When she finally spoke, her voice was low and venomous. "Do not recommend that horrible woman to anyone," she hissed. "Not if you care about your patients."

"Oh?" I said, feigning surprise. "You know the trainer?"

"*Hrpmh*. Trainer is not a word I would use to describe Dana Seller. 'Egomaniac' and 'someone who should be behind bars' is more like it." She crossed her arms over her chest. "Look, I don't know how much I can say considering the lawsuit, but that woman mistreated my poor Roxie. It's how we ended up at Pawsitive in the first place. I couldn't get far enough away from that monster."

"Did you say lawsuit?" I asked, trying not to appear too interested.

"Of course," Sara snapped. "I'm suing her for emotional damages to my sweet angel. My lawyer says we have an excellent case against her, and if all goes well, she will never be allowed to train another dog again."

There's little chance she can do that from the grave anyway, I thought.

As far as I could tell, the woman had every reason to hurt Dana, but I didn't think she had. For one, she truly didn't seem to know the dog trainer was dead.

She could have been acting, although I doubted Sara was a good enough actress to pull that off. Especially since she couldn't even stop herself from spilling the beans about the lawsuit, and I was certain her lawyer had advised her against it.

No, my gut said that while Sara obviously hated the dog trainer, she hadn't killed her.

"I'm sorry to hear you and Roxie had such a terrible experience. I appreciate your candor," I said. "I'll make sure to take her name off the list."

Sara huffed out what seemed to be a mix of frustration and relief. "Good. Was there anything else, or can I get back to Roxie? She gets a bit fidgety when she's alone."

From the porch, I caught sight of the ever calm Roxie burying her canines into an expensive-looking pillow and shaking it around until feathers snowed down around her.

"I think I'm all set. Thank you for your time."

With a curt nod, Sara ducked into the house, cooing, "Mommy's back."

Walking back toward my parked car, I tried to process the conversation. On the one hand, I was almost one hundred percent sure Sara was not involved in the death. On the other, something about her behavior struck me as odd.

Why divulge the information about the lawsuit? And if she was suing Dana, surely her lawyer would have informed her of the trainer's death. Not to mention someone at Pawsitive Academy could have passed on the message, since they must have known the history between the women when Sara had brought Roxie to them.

The story Sara had told me was almost too good. Too perfect.

I looked over my shoulder to find her watching me from the window. At her side, Roxie sat obediently, the exact opposite of the dog I'd witnessed a moment ago. My skin crawled. Something was off about Sara Cline, and I needed to find out what it was.

CHAPTER FOURTEEN

I hadn't been able to shake off my suspicions about Sara, so after my shift, I'd spent the next several hours aimlessly following her as she ran errands. First, she'd visited the nail salon, then she'd gone back to complain about a small chip and had it fixed. And by the time she'd visited the post office, stopped for a coffee and picked up her dry cleaning, I was beginning to think I'd wasted a perfectly good day off.

As I sat in the car across the street from Sara's house and watched her take grocery bags out of the trunk of her Range Rover, I realized it was time to call it a day. A yawn tugged at my lips and I turned to the side, my seat's reclined position making it impossible not to want to fall asleep. Outside, it had started to snow, and the fluffy flakes were piling up higher on my hood.

I moved to turn on the wipers, but stopped.

Sara had returned.

The woman wore a tight, insulated jogging outfit in deep navy blue that was designed to keep the chill out of your bones and the money out of your wallet. A matching beanie sat snug over her ears, and she pulled fleece-lined gloves onto her hands.

Roxie the poodle trotted beside her, bundled up in a little red sweater, booties, and a matching leash. The dog's curly fur stuck out around the edges of its coat, and its breath puffed into little clouds as they walked in step, both eager for whatever they had planned.

"Oh, no," I whispered. "Please, no."

My chest tightened as Sara took a sharp turn right on the street and headed toward the wooded area a few blocks away. If she was going jogging in this weather, I'd never keep up. Not only was I too tired to move my legs, but the idea of running was more nightmare inducing than swimming in a pool full of tarantulas.

To sum up: no, thank you.

A nagging thought tugged at my brain. What if she was about to do something illegal? I mean, sure, one could use the jogging trails for running, but there were plenty of things a person could do in the forest in the dead of winter.

Like bury a body, for example.

Not that Sara had one in tow with her. Still, it warranted further investigation. Maybe this wouldn't be a wasted day after all and I could go home with some peace of mind.

But how would I be able to follow her without being seen?

PUPS AND POISON

It was one thing to traipse around town in my car and follow the woman to public places; I could blend in easier there. Out here in the middle of nowhere, she was sure to spot me. Especially with my less-than-ninja-like movements.

My mother once told me that if she hadn't given birth to me, she'd have thought I was half-troll based on how much noise I made walking around. Not every vampire had to be an expert at sneaking around.

Then what was my plan?

I looked up and down the street, then at Sara's disappearing figure. If I was going to do this, I had to move fast. As much as I hated the idea, there was only one way I could follow her without being found out, and it involved using my least favorite vampire ability.

My teeth ground together as I pushed the button to raise the seat up.

Stepping from the car, my eyes darted right and left to make certain I was the only one around. I sucked in a deep lungful of the wintery air to calm my nerves and tapped into the transformation gene.

It took a bit of talking myself through it, but finally, my human body was gone and I was airborne. Flapping my tiny bat wings, I rose higher into the sky above the street.

My senses exploded as the abilities of my bat form rushed to the forefront and took control. A car honked several blocks away, the noise of it exploding in my head like a bomb. The sound ricocheted around my skull, causing my vision to blur briefly. Disoriented, I wobbled, drifting too far to the left.

I fixed my trajectory in seconds and flapped harder, heading the direction Sara had gone. The woman had quite the head start on me, but I could still spy glimpses of her bold jogging outfit through the trees.

Moving swiftly—and by swift, I mean awkwardly and without any grace—I darted through the forest to follow her. The large oaks rose around me, each one a threat I might face-plant into if I took a turn too sharp. Considering how out of practice I was at flying in bat form, I fared well enough. I caught up to Sara after a short while with my breath only slightly hitching.

Suddenly, she stopped in her tracks. Her move was so abrupt, I had to bank hard to the left to find a hiding place so she wouldn't get freaked out about a bat rustling around over her head.

Settling onto the branch of a nearby tree, I tucked in my wings and watched. Far below me, Sara moved to the far side of the trail and pulled out a cellphone.

Her voice rose as she answered, annoyance lacing her words. "Hey there. It's my day off. I can't speak for long."

At her feet, Roxie wagged her tail, then growled.

"Oh. It's you," Sara said, her tone darkening. "Right now? Fine. But I don't see why this couldn't wait until tomorrow. I'll meet you there within the hour. I had to come down, anyway; this will save me the trip."

She hung up and shoved the phone into a hidden pocket in her pants. Bending down to pat Roxie on the head, she let out a long, frustrated groan before marching back the way she'd come.

A few feet down the path, Sara broke into a jog and I sputtered, hurrying to take flight. This time, I couldn't keep up with her ever-quickening pace. The woman was running so fast she was practically floating above the ground.

If I'd attempted to keep pace with her, there was a high likelihood her healthy lifestyle would have killed me. As it was, I didn't think I'd be able to lift my arms the next day.

Slowing down, I reached the line separating the forest from the main road, with Sara only a dot on the horizon in front of me. Based on her trajectory, it was obvious she was going back home, so there was no point in hurrying. As long as I got to my car before she left again, I was safe.

Taking my time, I flew down the empty street, keeping watch so I didn't scare a passerby. When I reached the car, I ducked behind it, collected myself, and allowed the transformation to take over.

My bones creaked as the magic that allowed me to take bat form returned to the deep crevices of my body, and I was once again standing on two legs. Sliding into the back-seat, I dressed, hoping no one spotted me and called the cops, thinking I was an exhibitionist.

Once I finished, I crawled over the middle console and settled myself behind the wheel. Then I waited. And waited. And waited.

Hadn't Sara said she'd see whoever was on the other side of the phone call in one hour?

I looked at the clock on the dash, my brow furrowing. It

has been an hour and twenty minutes since she'd left the jogging trails. Either Sara hadn't gone home to change, or she was running late. And since she didn't strike me as someone who would dare show up to any appointment in a sweaty jogging suit, the latter seemed more likely.

My eyes narrowed on the large house at the end of the long driveway. Unless she was dressing for the red carpet, it shouldn't have taken this long. What if she'd snuck out the back of her house instead of taking her car?

Groaning in frustration, I got out of the car, gently closing the door without slamming it and slunk down the driveway toward Sara's front door. Unable to help myself, I continuously searched around and behind me on the off chance I was being watched. But every time I checked, no one was around.

If I was right and Sara was long gone, it left her home empty. Save for Roxie possibly hanging around, but I doubted she'd leave her precious princess alone.

I wasn't going to break in, of course. The plan was to see what I could spy through the gargantuan windows that lined the entire building. Luckily, Sara wasn't particularly concerned with privacy because none of the windows were covered by blinds or curtains. She didn't even have one of those fancy video doorbells.

Feet padding across the ground, I skirted around the house and pressed my nose to the glass pane of a side window. All I saw was an empty hallway with closed doors on either side.

There was a large abstract painting in black and white

on the far wall, and several olive trees were planted in giant pots around it. Walking around to the back of the house, I took in Sara's backyard, which was as impressive as the front. I spotted a covered pool, a small greenhouse, and what appeared to be a guest cottage painted in pastel lilac with decorative white shutters.

I was about to head back toward the front yard when a loud crash pierced the silent air around me. My head twisted around to face the door, heart jumping into my throat.

Something had fallen inside the house. Hard.

Going against my better judgment, I reached out and pulled on the sliding door.

Please be locked, please be locked... I begged, wanting a reason to sprint toward my car and get the heck out of there.

It was unlocked.

The glass slid to the side and heat from inside the house blasted me in the face. Sara must have put the fireplace on because my retinas felt as though they were quite literally burning.

"Sara?" I took a tentative step inside.

What was I going to say if I came face to face with her? *"Hi! I wanted to speak to you about your car's extended warranty?"*

I mentally face-palmed. Sara didn't seem to have the best sense of humor.

No answer.

"Sara? Is everything okay?"

This time, my words were met with loud, panicked barking. The type of barking that said something was terribly wrong. Was Roxie hurt?

Not thinking twice, I took off in a sprint toward the sound. My legs felt like liquid, but I kept on until I reached Roxie standing at the top of a staircase landing. The dog continued to bark, her wide, panicked eyes darting between me and the doorway in front of her.

Relieved to see she appeared to be uninjured, I stepped closer and peered down the set of stairs that led to the basement.

"It's all right, girl." I petted her between the ears to calm her down, but it didn't help. "What's going—"

My mouth dried and my heart tripped over its beat as terror clawed its way up my spine. There, at the bottom of the stairs, lay a crumpled body. I swallowed the saliva that pooled in my mouth and lowered myself into a crouch so I could cradle Roxie against me. Surprisingly, the dog didn't fight or protest my touch.

We sat huddled at the top of the stairs, our horrified focus on Sara. The woman had fallen down the stairs. There was no question about it. And from the looks of it, it had been a bad fall.

Sara wasn't moving.

Or breathing.

I didn't need to go down to check to know for certain, but I did so anyway. On trembling legs, I rose, telling Roxie to stay put while I made my way shakily downstairs.

Kneeling beside her, I checked for a pulse, confirming what I already knew.

Sara Cline was dead.

A banging on the door interrupted my racing thoughts.

My gaze met Roxie's. "Who could that be?" I asked the dog.

The second knock was louder and more urgent, forcing me to leave Sara's side and stomp up the stairs toward the front of the house. Roxie stayed where she was, whining as she watched over her owner.

My heart broke for the poodle. *No pet should outlive their best friend.*

As fast as I could manage, I unlocked the bolts on the front door and opened it wide. My stomach sank.

Standing on the front steps was none other than Officer Baggard. His hat was pulled down low, casting a dark shadow over his even darker eyes.

"Miss Pane," he said gruffly, focusing his disapproving gaze on me. "What are you doing here? I need to speak to Sara Cline immediately. It is urgent."

I winced. "About that…"

CHAPTER FIFTEEN

"You expect me to believe that you just happened to show up at the exact moment the victim fell down the stairs?" Officer Baggard asked, not bothering to hide his disbelief. "And you didn't see it happen?"

I shook my head. "No. I heard Roxie and came running, but it was too late."

"Roxie?"

"The dog, officer," I said, exasperated. "As I've said several times already, she was barking frantically. I'm a veterinarian and I was concerned she needed medical attention. The sound led me to the top of the stairs, which was when I saw Sara lying there."

The young man scribbled furiously in a small notebook. His pen wobbled, and he strained to keep his writing on the tiny sheets of paper. *Why not get a bigger book?*

I guessed Officer Baggard was trying to emulate the detectives he saw on television. It was ridiculous, and at this slow pace, I'd be lucky to make it home before sundown. Talk about a crappy day off.

Baggard's nose twitched, and he let out a loud, open-mouthed sneeze. I jumped back a little, barely avoiding the spit that sprayed from his mouth.

He wiped them, his eyes red and watery. "Is someone burning incense in here?"

I sniffed the air. "I don't think so. Why?"

"I'm deathly allergic to the stuff." He grimaced at his choice of words, recovering quickly by tossing another angry glare my way. "You mentioned the door was open when you arrived?"

I nodded. "The side door, yes. I didn't check the front door."

He looked up, his eyes narrowing. "Why didn't you use the front if you were visiting?"

Hmm. I had to give it to him, that was a very good question, and one I couldn't answer without getting myself into further trouble. How was I supposed to convince the officer that I wasn't there to hurt Sara when I'd been skulking around her property like a complete creep?

There was no way he would believe I had no ill intentions if I tried to explain that I was only there to gather evidence. For him. The last thing I needed was for Archie to think I believed him incapable of doing his job.

Which I did, but that was neither here nor there.

I settled on saying only what was absolutely necessary

and flashed him what I hoped was a disarming smile. "I didn't want to knock down her art piece on the front walkway. I nearly destroyed it yesterday, and Sara wasn't pleased about it."

"The pile of rocks?"

I cringed. "Yes. The rocks."

"Right," the officer said, still unconvinced. "What about once you were inside the premises? Did you see anyone else around?"

Anyone else? What was going on here? Did Archie think there was foul play involved?

I saw nothing that might have implied Sara hadn't tripped and fallen when I'd come in, but I hadn't exactly been paying attention, what with Roxie barking like she'd gone mad and then finding Sara, well, dead.

My thoughts raced as I tried to recall the scene when I'd entered. I remembered running through the house to reach the dog, but little else came to mind.

There had been a breeze in the air... Was there a window open somewhere in the house? Could someone have possibly used it to escape after pushing Sara down the basement stairs?

It was impossible to tell, considering how spotty my memories of the last hour were.

"I can't say for certain." I looked back at Archie Baggard. "As far as I could tell, she fell."

"Down her own stairs?" the officer asked, slowly turning the page in his book. "Stairs she walked up and down every day she lived in this house?"

Was that sarcasm?

I didn't appreciate his tone, or where his mind seemed to be going.

Brushing back my curls, I pressed my lips into a thin line and set my jaw. "Am I free to leave now, officer?"

"I'm afraid not, Miss Pane." Archie pointed to the door with his pen. "I have some more questions for you. Ones I'd like to ask down at the station. Please follow me there."

I gulped. *Oh, brother.*

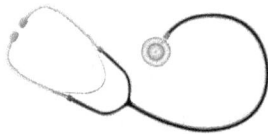

As it turned out, Officer Baggard's idea of bringing me in for questioning included shoving me in an empty room and leaving for over an hour. Probably so he could go watch a few episodes of his favorite detective TV series so he could make notes about what to ask a murder suspect.

I rested my elbows on the metal table and tried not to notice the loops built into the top to accommodate hand-cuffs. It was impossible to do, since they were the only detail in the room unless you counted the slight crack in the two-way mirror in front of me. My eyes flicked around the boxy room I'd been deposited in.

The whitewashed cement walls had paint peeling off, giving it a weathered patina look—not the chic kind that DIY influencers tried to achieve with sponging, either. It was more along the lines of a we-haven't-washed-these-walls-in-decades look. The only thing in worse condition than the walls were the torn leather chairs that no longer had any cushioning or support.

Seriously, I was going to need a visit to the chiropractor if I spent another minute on the dreadful thing. And humans had the gall to believe coffins were uncomfortable? At least they were lined in silk and fluffy cushions.

I was really over this entire day. My throat was parched, since the junior officer hadn't bothered to offer me water while I waited, although it wasn't the type of liquid I needed, anyway. Not to mention I was beyond exhausted.

If Archie's plan was to bring me to the point of complete irritation to get me to talk, there was a good chance it would work. At this point, I would have admitted to burying bodies in my backyard if it meant getting me out of this room.

As if he could read my thoughts, the metal door creaked to open, revealing a narrow-eyed Officer Baggard. The young man strolled toward the second chair in the room, slowly dragging it away from the table. The sound of metal on tile made my skin crawl.

With a huff, he lowered himself into the seat and glared at me.

"So…" I said, my voice scratchy and dry. "You said you have questions to ask me?"

The officer cleared his throat. "I did. But it appears that you're off the hook."

I was so confused.

"Off the hook for what?" I asked, baffled. "I told you

everything that happened. To be honest, I'm not sure why I'm here at all."

"You were the first on the scene at two deaths, both of which could have been connected."

Despite my exhaustion, my lips twisted into a grin. "*Ah-ha!* So you do believe there was foul play in Dana's death?" I thought back to the staircase. "But Sara fell, right? How could they be connected? What am I missing?"

"You are not missing anything, Miss Pane. Let me remind you that, unlike some of the other detectives, I am not comfortable with a civilian getting involved in ongoing investigations. Especially ones with a record for weak alibis."

"I'm sorry, what?" My eyes bulged out of my head. "Why would I need an alibi? You literally saw me. If you think I had anything to do with the deaths of those two women, why would I bother sticking around? I could have left the park instead of calling Detective Wolff and reporting that Dana's body had been found."

The officer shut his mouth, and a muscle in his jaw ticked. He rubbed his eyes with the fleshy part of his palms. When he finally looked at me again, I could see the disdain he felt for me as clear as day.

"I don't know why you did what you did," Archie sneered. "But I want you to know that I am watching you, Miss Pane. I would tread lightly from here on out. Your friends in high places won't always be around to bail you out."

He pushed the chair back, making the metal legs grind

into the tile. I winced, my sensitive eardrums vibrating in pain from the chair's shriek of protest.

Continuing to glare at me, he stood up and marched to the door. He opened it with more force than was necessary and gave me one final glance before stepping out into the corridor and stomping away.

Who in the name of Bram Stoker had shoved a stake up the man's butt?

A second later, another face popped into the doorway.

In the space of a heartbeat, my pulse slowed, and the stress of the day dissipated.

"Ryder! You're back!" I beamed up at him, unable to hide my joy.

"Sure am," Ryder responded warmly. "Got in an hour ago. I was going to text you, but a friend called to tell me Archie had dragged you into the station. I thought I'd swing by and see what kind of trouble you'd gotten yourself into this time."

"Am I glad to see you! I thought I was going to sleep behind bars tonight."

Ryder chuckled, the sound making my stomach flutter. "That would never happen. Archie tends to get ahead of himself, but his heart is in the right place."

"He thinks I killed Dana," I grumbled, scowling out the door in the direction Baggard had gone. "And Sara too."

I looked back at Ryder just in time to see a flicker of darkness flash through his eyes. There was a storm gathering in their depths that sent a pang of worry through me.

I frowned. "What aren't you telling me?"

Ryder motioned to the corridor with his chin, his wide frame obscuring the view entirely. "Let's talk somewhere else. I'm sure you're eager to get home, and I can't wait to see Benny. If you don't mind some company, that is."

"Not at all," I said. "But we'll need to swing by the clinic. Benny had so much fun with two dogs we're boarding for the next week that I left him there for the day with Grennich and Bree."

I just hoped Grennich had been able to reverse the effects of her spell on Benny while I'd been investigating Sara.

With a nod from Ryder, I stood up and followed him out of the room and toward the front of the station. As we passed Officer Baggard, I kept my eyes straight ahead, refusing to give him a chance to intimidate me.

Archie may have had a badge and a vendetta against me, but I had something much better.

I looked at Ryder's muscled back as he stalked out of the station.

I had a werewolf on my side.

CHAPTER SIXTEEN

A fter stopping by the clinic to pick up a no-longer-glowing Benny, we headed to my house. I parked and waited until Ryder pulled his car up behind mine to kill the engine and step out.

As soon as my eyes landed on the front door of my home, my stomach sank. The door was wide open, and even from here, I could see where someone had used brute force to bust the lock. Dread clawed at my chest as I stood frozen, unable to pull my gaze from the house.

Someone had broken into my home.

"Stay behind me," Ryder ordered, stepping around me.

Before I could register what was going on, his police-issued gun was in his hands, pointed at the open door. After what had gone down in the deserted warehouse when I'd been investigating Polly and Justin's deaths, seeing another gun was unnerving, but this was Ryder, and he knew what he was doing.

Besides, if someone was still in my house, it would be much better if they came face to face with a highly trained police detective, rather than a scared vamp who might or might not turn into a bat on the spot.

Ryder moved through the doorway with his gun raised, and I followed slowly behind him. As my eyes adjusted to the dim interior, I caught my breath, taking in the familiar surroundings that suddenly felt incredibly foreign.

Behind us, Benny let out a bark, and I glanced over my shoulder to make sure he was still safe in the front seat of Ryder's car. Satisfied he was okay, I stepped further inside.

The cozy, decorated entrance hallway that usually welcomed me home seemed to close in around us. Shadows stretched across the walls from the light filtering through the glass panels by the door, and eerie shapes danced across the hardwood floor as we walked further in. Every creak of the old house seemed amplified, like it was trying to tell us what had happened during my absence.

Ryder advanced slowly, his stance calm and steady, but there was a sharp edge in his gaze as he scanned every corner and cranny. I followed behind him, acutely aware that we might not be alone. The idea of a stranger some-where within these walls made my stomach twist, but if anyone was lurking here, they were about to have a very bad night.

Rolling my shoulders, I gritted my teeth and gave

myself a mental shake. I was a vampire—one of the most feared paranormal species on Earth.

If they wanted a fight, they could come and get me!

A loud bang had me screaming and fighting the urge to leap onto Ryder's back.

On second thought, please leave me alone.

Ryder motioned for me to hang back and disappeared into the belly of my house. He moved toward the sound, and I didn't realize until the room started to blur and spin that at some point, I'd stopped breathing.

There was more banging, followed by a storm of cursing from Ryder. A second later, wings flapped overhead as Byrd zipped out of wherever he'd been hiding and flew past me and into the kitchen. My gaze followed the bat as it settled into one of his favorite spots next to a display bowl of fake fruit.

Shortly after, Ryder emerged, his gun holstered.

"It's clear. No one's here," he said. His chin jerked toward a sulking Byrd. "A little warning about the bat next time."

I furrowed my brow. "Hopefully, this will be the only time someone breaks into my house. But sure, I'll warn you next time."

"Do you see anything missing?"

I twisted around, giving the house a quick inspection, but from what I could see, everything was as it should be. I held up a finger and moved to open a few drawers.

"Not a thing," I replied, slamming them shut. "Why would someone break in and not take anything?"

My words fell on deaf ears because Ryder was no longer listening. He had his nose up in the air and was sniffing like he was at the holiday display of cologne at the department store. The more he sniffed, the brighter his eyes glowed.

Unable to take it anymore, I did the only thing I could think of: I joined the weirdo. The second I took one big whiff of the air, my entire body broke into goosebumps.

Alarmed, I squeaked, "Is… Is that—"

"Supernatural. It's light, but it's there," he said. "Whoever broke into your house, they were one of us."

All the moisture in my mouth evaporated, turning it drier than the Sahara. What did a supe need so badly from my house that they'd break in to get it?

I did a third scan of the premises, struggling to figure out why they'd commit a crime, but not take a single thing for their efforts. There wasn't even a chair overturned. What was going on?

Could this be connected to Dana's death? Was someone unhappy that I was digging around?

No, that didn't make any sense.

Dana was human.

I looked at Ryder and sucked in a bated breath. "What am I missing? Could this be related to Sara or Dana somehow?"

"There was nothing supernatural about Sara's death; one of the crime scene techs is a supe and would have alerted me. There are signs that what happened to the dog trainer wasn't an accident, though."

"I knew it!" I hissed. "What gave it away?"

Once more, the same darkness I'd witnessed in the police station flashed across his face. "I pushed some buttons while I was gone and had another detective look in on Baggard's work. He found inconsistencies in the autopsy that didn't align with a choking case. A tox report has been requested, but because it's not my case—or my friend's— we had to wait for Baggard to approve it."

"No wonder he was so mad," I whispered. "What did the report say?"

"It hasn't come back yet. But our request was enough to light a fire under Baggard, and he took extra care with Sara Cline's investigation. He found evidence of a break in."

I pointed a thumb at my chest, raising an eyebrow in an unspoken question.

"No, not you," Ryder said, shaking his head. "He hoped it was you, but there was clear evidence that someone was there before you. The alarm at the back door was tampered with and the lock was broken. Since you came in through the side, Archie had to rule you out. He was not happy about it."

"Why is he so keen on making me a suspect?" I huffed.

Ryder rolled his eyes skyward. "I don't think it's personal. He wants to close the case faster to make himself look better. The kid is competitive, which is great, but he can't be cutting corners. That's not the job. I also think he felt I was looking over his shoulder, and he took it out on you. Don't take it to heart."

"Hard to do that when I'm being hauled in to get interrogated," I said. "Anyway, let's go get Benny. The poor fella is probably going stir crazy in your car."

As we marched toward the front door, the hairs on the back of my neck prickled, refusing to settle. The air was thick, pressing down on me with a suffocating weight, as if each step I took was through a dense bog. Breathing felt like pulling wet wool through my lungs, and every creak of the floor seemed amplified, echoing in the quiet that had settled over the house.

Even if nothing had been stolen, I still couldn't help but feel violated. No amount of changing the locks would make this fear go away. I needed to get better protection for my home, but I had no idea what could help make me feel safer inside.

Everywhere I looked, I was reminded that someone else had been in here. Someone I hadn't invited.

I reached for Benny's leash on the narrow shelf above the key hooks. As my hand brushed against it, a faint rustle broke the silence. An envelope slipped from the edge of the shelf and fluttered to the floor.

I stopped cold, my breath hitching as I stared down at it.

The envelope was unassuming at first glance—a plain white slip in plain paper. In bold, stark lettering, two words were stamped across the front, perfectly centered:

Ophelia Pane.

My name stared back at me, and a lump formed in my throat.

"What's that?" Ryder asked.

Since I hadn't the slightest idea, I didn't answer. Instead,

I bent down and snatched the envelope up, inspecting the paper before ripping the seam open. With shaking fingers, I pulled out the thick card tucked inside.

Blood rushed between my ears, and the sound of it made my head hurt. My heart raced, pounding at my ribcage with the force of a hurricane. I bit the inside of my cheek and looked at Ryder.

"A warning," I whispered. "Whoever broke in, this is what they came here to do. They're sending us a message."

"What do they want?"

My legs trembled, and I leaned against the wall to steady myself. "Turn in the hellhound or else."

CHAPTER SEVENTEEN

A fter several cups of tea for Ryder, and two blood juice boxes for me, we both relaxed—at least enough to think about what had happened rationally. We sat on my couch, the front door solidly locked with a chair in front of it courtesy of yours truly, and tried to come up with a plan.

Hiding Benny was clearly no longer working. Whoever was after him knew Ryder had left the puppy with me, which meant we were both being watched, so stashing him away at the clinic was out of the question. As was hiding him from anyone who worked there.

I hated that we'd inadvertently painted a bullseye on Bree and Grennich's backs, but we didn't exactly have much of a choice here. Besides, both women had fallen in love with the pup, and they'd been more than willing to help keep him away from the SJD.

There was also the matter of my little situation with Officer Baggard. Somehow, I doubted he'd be letting me off the hook easily, especially after his comment about my friends not being able to protect me forever. Not to mention the power play Ryder had pulled at the station by walking in and demanding my release.

"We should focus on clearing your name before Baggard goes overboard and does something foolish," Ryder said, rubbing his forehead as though trying to ease a headache.

I crossed my legs, curling myself into as tiny a ball as possible. "No way. Let's figure this thing out with Benny, then we can worry about me."

"As much as I'd love to find a way to help Benny, we don't know who we're dealing with or how they even found out about him. Nor do we have any clue on what to do about it."

I blew out a frustrated breath. He was right.

"So we should focus on the problem we can control," Ryder reasoned. "The case you're implicated in."

"Falsely implicated," I corrected. "And fine. What are you thinking?"

There was a short pause while Ryder lifted his tea and downed what was left in one long go. When he put the mug down, it was empty but still steaming.

Raking his fingers through his thick hair, he pinned me with his watchful gaze. "I'd like to give the dog academy owner another go."

"Karen?" I asked, my eyebrows hiking up higher. "She clamped up tight when I was there. It was pretty suspicious, but maybe she simply wasn't interested in talking to me."

"Maybe she'd be more willing to talk if she knew a detective was asking," Ryder mused.

"Very true. And you're attractive, so that can't hurt." Realizing what I'd blurted out, I rushed ahead without giving him a chance to speak. "Plus, she knew both victims, which makes it well worth looking into."

Karen hadn't simply known both victims; she may have had a hand in their deaths. Emphasis on *may*. All I really had to base my theory on was her absolutely bizarre behavior when I'd visited, but it was enough for me. If you weren't guilty of something, why act like you were?

But what was her motive in murdering the women if she was the killer?

Dana's death was easier to guess at—the competition of the business and her general dislike for the dog trainer's practices. If Karen held even half the beliefs that Sara had about the harsh methods the trainer used, it could have pushed her over the edge to take matters into her own hands.

But Sara's death didn't make any sense. From what I'd gathered, the women got along well, and Sara had been a perfect client who'd written hefty checks for things like puppy poetry.

Unless Karen's niece didn't know the full story about what had gone down with Sara and Dana and there was more to it.

I scratched my head, groaning audibly. Ryder was right.

The only way to get to the bottom of this was to try talking to her again.

"How about we go there tomorrow morning? First thing when they open," I suggested.

"Sounds like a plan to me," Ryder agreed. "Now, if you don't mind, I think I'll sleep on your couch tonight in case whoever was here comes back."

"Safety in numbers." I smiled. "Let me get you a pillow and some blankets."

For the rest of the night, I tried to ignore the flutter in my stomach each time I remembered the werewolf sleeping in my living room. As far as I was concerned, I couldn't have been safer.

WITNESSING Ryder's reaction when we pulled up to Pawsitive Academy was worth making the drive, even if we learned nothing helpful while there. His jaw went slack, and he rubbed his temples in an attempt to make sense of the place. If I hadn't been here before and experienced the same shock of seeing the sprawling estate, I'd have been ogling the academy right alongside him.

I pulled my car into the lot, relieved to find it empty. Since we arrived at the crack of dawn, I assumed the place wouldn't be busy yet, but one never knew what to expect. My experience with dog training, especially the uppity kind, was minimal. For all I knew, Karen was over here running a sunrise doggy origami class or a pancakes for puppies cooking class.

"This is a dog training place?" Ryder asked as he stepped out of the car.

I laughed. "I know. It's massive, huh?"

"It looks like it could be an entire camp. Or a wedding venue." He looked at the wood cabin before us and let out a low whistle. "Lead the way."

We made our way around the side of the building to the same entrance I'd used last time. The snow had covered most of the walkway overnight, and I took careful steps, trying to stay balanced since I wasn't wearing my winter boots.

Knowing my luck, I'd end up with my butt in the air if I wasn't careful... especially with Ryder here. Life had a tendency to embarrass me when I least needed it to.

Not that I cared about impressing the detective or anything.

I slowed down, placing my foot down on the first step up the porch. The ice hadn't yet formed, so luckily, I didn't go flying off immediately.

Ryder followed close behind me, using the same amount of caution, although I was pretty sure that was for my sake. Werewolves had notoriously exceptional balance, and if Ryder did somehow manage to trip, he could probably snap his claws out in time to steady himself.

I, on the other hand, was not so great at vamping out

when I needed a supernatural assist, thus the white-knuck-ling of the railing I was currently taking part in.

Reaching the door, I pushed it open and quickly stepped inside. The reception area looked exactly the same as it had on my last visit, except today there was no sign of Karen's niece and there wasn't a dog anywhere in the vicinity.

"It's quiet," Ryder noted.

I shrugged. "Probably because it's still early. I'm sure Karen's in the back, setting up for poetry or 'pawsome painting.' This was as far as I got last time. Why don't you lead the way? I doubt she'll appreciate seeing my face first thing this morning."

"She'd be a fool not to," Ryder said, his smile warm.

My skin flushed at the compliment and I instantly averted my gaze, suddenly finding the wooden plank walls of the cabin super interesting. Walking behind Ryder, I took note of every framed photograph we passed, each one a depiction of a happy dog. I assumed they were all previous or current customers of Karen's.

The hallway opened to another large area ahead of us where several armchairs nestled around a central coffee table. On the table sat three large bowls. One held doggy treats, the other natural snack bars for the owners, and a larger bowl with a mix of other necessities one might have needed while waiting for their dog's training session to end.

There were small packets of gum and mints, mini water bottles, several tubes of lip balm, and prepack-aged toothpicks. I noticed the lip balm was the same brand as the one I'd seen Dana use at the dog park and made a note of it to check it out later to see what all the fuss was about. Knowing Karen, it was probably all natural.

Next to several baskets filled with balls was a collection of crystals laid out in a circle and a miniature Zen Garden, complete with a tiny rake.

"Interesting place," Ryder said.

I snickered. "You have no idea."

"You're back, I see." The air turned frigid as Karen walked into the room.

In her right hand, she held another bowl of random things that she added to the collection on the table. I fought the urge to laugh.

How many giveaway items did the woman need to palm off on her customers? No wonder people enjoyed this place. It was like a department store in here.

Across from us, Karen's eyes gave me a dismissive once over, then landed on Ryder. "And you brought a friend," she said, her voice warming and taking on a slight southern drawl. "Am I to assume you're not here for dog training, either?"

"Afraid not," Ryder replied. He reached into his jacket and pulled out his badge, flashing it at Karen.

The sickly sweet smile she was giving him melted away instantly.

"Detective Ryder Wolff. I'm here to ask you a few questions about Sara Cline."

It was so quiet you could hear a penny drop as her mouth opened and closed like a fish out of water. Finally, she managed to ask, "I thought you were here about Dana?"

"How would you describe your client, Sara Cline?" Ryder asked, ignoring her statement.

"Um, normal, I guess. A dedicated dog parent," Karen said, her forehead creasing. "Why?"

"Have you noticed any change in her behavior the last few weeks? Did she seem like something was bothering her?" Ryder asked, ignoring her question.

"What's going on, detective?" Karen asked. Her confusion was slowly giving way to irritation. "Is Sara all right?"

"I'm afraid I can't get into it at the moment, but I would appreciate it if you could answer a few more questions. Did Sara appear to be on edge? Perhaps afraid?"

Karen's face grew ashen, and a vein pulsed on her forehead. She sucked in a shaky breath, her body nearly crumbling as she lowered into the cushions of the couch closest to her.

All her brusque confidence vanished and her teeth chattered as she spoke again. "S-She's not okay, is she?"

When Ryder didn't answer, she closed her eyes and sighed. "I knew she was going to get herself in over her head. I just knew it. I told her to get help, but she refused to listen and it wasn't my place to intervene."

"What do you mean?" I asked, moving to sit in the chair across from her.

"Sara was a wonderful person. Truly a gem and the best client anyone could ask for," Karen said. "When she came to us after her trouble with Dana, we grew close. Developed a friendship, really. It was probably why she felt comfortable opening up to me."

Ryder crossed his arms. "About what, exactly?"

"Her gambling addiction," Karen said point blank. "Sara was in too deep and she had no idea how to get out. I told her so many times to walk away, to speak to a professional before she lost everything she owned, but she never went through with it. It was bad, detective. Really bad."

The pitch of Ryder's voice lowered to a deep rumble. "Did she owe money?"

Karen nodded, her eyes downcast. "After a while, she stopped sharing details with me, but I knew something was wrong." She glanced at me briefly before settling on Ryder again. "If Sara got into some sort of trouble, I'm sure it was because of her... problem."

For a moment, I thought Ryder was going to grill her more, but he nodded and took a few steps back. My eyes widened in confusion. There was so much more I wanted to ask the academy owner.

Like who did Sara owe money to and would they stoop so low as to kill her to get it? How much money were we talking about? Did people really use toothpicks during a meditation class?

As I said, I had many, many questions.

Unfortunately, Ryder was not going to give me any time to ask them. He thanked Sara and left her his card in case she thought of anything else. Then he turned on his heel and marched us out the same way we'd come in.

When we stepped outside and the door closed behind

me, I let out an aggravated groan. "Why didn't you ask more questions?"

Ryder shook his head. "I'm not even technically supposed to be here," he said. "If I asked her anything else, I'd have to tell her Sara Cline died, and she'd be running straight to the station next. We can't risk that. If we want to clear your name and figure out what happened to both Dana and Sara, we need to keep our heads down and not draw Baggard's attention."

"I suppose that makes sense," I said. "But how do we find out who Sara owed money to?"

The detective wiggled his bushy brows. "I happen to know just the person for that."

While he stomped through the snow to the car, I turned to get one final look at the academy. Something gnawed at me that I couldn't quite pinpoint, a twisting in my stomach that told me things were not as they seemed, except I had no idea what had me feeling so unsettled.

A curtain fluttered in one of the second-story windows and I squinted in time to see a familiar silhouette disappear from view.

Karen was watching us. But why? What did the academy owner know that she wasn't sharing?

I zipped my coat up and walked away slowly. There was only one way to find out. Hopefully, Ryder had an ace up his sleeve he was waiting to use. One that would help us crack this case wide open.

CHAPTER EIGHTEEN

I f I had to guess who a Bluejay Falls detective might have tapped as a resource to help solve a possible murder, it would never have been the woman sitting before me. My stomach lurched as soon as she walked into the bistro Ryder had arranged for us to meet her in, and my stress level rose with each step the mermaid took toward our table.

Around me, the sounds of plates clinking and people placing their orders for fancy sandwiches and onion soup faded into the background. All I could concentrate on was the shiny golden hair swinging behind the woman's back— hair that reached all the way to her knees.

I knew this mermaid.

"Something the matter?" Ryder asked, no doubt reading my disgruntled expression.

"That's your source?"

He nodded, and I frowned. The mermaid was the same one who'd interviewed for our vacant vet tech position before we'd hired Grennich. The one who'd turned my clinic upside down to teach the werewolf a lesson after he'd scorned her.

Was our town truly so small that this had to be Ryder's infinite source of information? How did he know her? They hadn't even acted like they knew each other when he'd stopped by with Benny.

And what could a mermaid possibly know about the world of gambling and loan sharks?

The woman sauntered over to us and slid her shapely hourglass figure into an empty seat. She was beautiful, and I couldn't help but wonder if they'd dated.

Her lips curled into a knowing grin when she saw me sitting next to Ryder. Keeping her large blue eyes on me, she dropped a designer purse on the table.

"Hello again, detective," she said. "I hope we can make it quick. I'm due back at the casino in an hour."

Oh. My skin blushed at the Olympic-level jumping to conclusions I'd done before. Besides, it wasn't my business who he dated.

Her resume hadn't mentioned that she currently worked at a casino, but now it made sense that she might have information Ryder could use.

I feigned a smile and tried to appear more welcoming. "Thanks for meeting us, Morgana," I said. "I didn't realize you worked at the casino when you interviewed with us."

"You know each other?" Ryder asked, his eyebrows drawing together.

"Barely," Morgana replied. She flicked her long hair over her shoulder and it landed an inch away from Ryder's bowl of soup. "I applied for a vet tech position at her clinic. Didn't get it."

Don't forget how you trashed the place. My smile faltered.

"Ah, all right. That makes sense," Ryder said.

I guess he'd been so caught up in how to ask for his favor and in helping me clean, he hadn't paid attention to what Bree had been doing with the two applicants.

Regardless, I was having a very hard time understanding what skillset the mermaid actually possessed. Considering the list of jobs on her current resume, which hadn't even included the casino, she was either a Jack of All Trades or someone who was desperate for work. No matter how I spun it, I couldn't make sense of why this specific woman was Ryder's informant.

Across from me, Morgana chuckled under her breath. "I understand people," she said. "That's why he needs me."

I choked on my own saliva.

"Y-You can read minds?"

Morgana shrugged. "To a degree. It's a latent mermaid trait that, back in the day, allowed us to communicate underwater. No one really lives below shore anymore though, which is why it's becoming a rare ability," she explained. "But it makes for a nifty trick, especially when dealing cards. As for the clinic, I'm also decent at understanding animals. That was why I applied."

"Oh," I said, fully embarrassed now. "That would have been a handy ability to have around."

"I know."

The awkward silence between us stretched on for what seemed like forever. I tried not to stare at Morgana, but the mermaid had an appeal that made it hard to look away.

If the clinic was in a less frugal financial situation, I would have asked her to come back for a more thorough interview. I'd meant what I said—her ability to read the minds of the animals would've made for an excellent addition. Perhaps I could have taken her on as a part-time assistant for the more difficult cases...

I started to say something but stopped myself. It was best that I didn't make any decisions without consulting Bree and Grennich. I might have been the owner, but our little team was working well, and I didn't want to rock the boat.

"I need some information on a case that involved a frequent flyer at the casino," Ryder said, preventing me from doing something rash. "Think you can help me out?"

The mermaid grinned. A mischievous glint sparked in her eyes as she leaned her elbows on the table and slid closer to Ryder. "For the right price."

"Of course," Ryder agreed. "What can you tell me about Sara Cline?"

The mermaid flinched, her eyes widening. She stood from the table without uttering another word and zipped up her long puffer jacket all the way to her chin. Then she spun around and started for the door.

Beside me, Ryder rolled his eyes and took out his phone, clicking away rapidly. I watched, confused, as Morgana's cellphone pinged a few feet away from us. She stopped her stride to glance down at the screen, her shoulders lifting.

A second later, she spun back around and marched to the table with a sneer on her face. "You better send double that amount." She slammed her phone on the table. "Cline was bad news, and I'll be risking my neck—and tail—if I talk to you about her."

"Done," Ryder agreed. "Now, what is it about this woman that makes you so afraid? We've been working together for years and this is the first time I've seen you even consider walking away without getting paid. You never turn down money."

"You don't understand! Sara Cline wasn't simply a patron of the casino," the mermaid snapped. "She owed the big boss a ton of cash. We're talking about buy-yourself-a-mansion kind of money."

Ryder leaned back against the booth. "What about her loan shark?"

"There was no loan shark," Morgana said. "Cline borrowed straight from the house. She knew the boss from back in the day and he offered her a friends-and-family deal. A low interest loan that kept her coming back."

"I'm assuming since you're using past tense, you heard she died?" I asked.

The mermaid nodded curtly. "It's been all anyone could talk—or think—about since it happened."

"What does your boss think of it all?" Ryder drummed his fingers on the table.

"No clue. I haven't seen him in weeks." She shrugged again and settled into the seat once more. "His goons are still around and watching the place, but Mikey has been off on back-to-back business trips. But if you're sniffing around for foul play in Cline's death, I'd steer clear."

"Why's that?" Ryder asked.

"Mikey always gets what he's owed," she replied. She bit her bottom lip. "One way or another, they pay. Either with cash or with their life. I wouldn't be surprised if that's what happened to Cline too. No one would be."

She shifted uncomfortably, crossing and uncrossing her legs a few times before giving up and standing again. Glancing from me to Ryder, she tapped her phone with a bright red fingernail. "I'll be expecting the rest of the deposit before I start my car. Good doing business with you, detective."

With those final words, Morgana left the restaurant without a backward glance. I watched Ryder fiddle with his phone, transferring the remainder of her payment. All the while, my thoughts were rushing a mile a minute.

Why was I not buying the explanation Morgana had given us?

"Well, that settles it," Ryder said, oblivious to my inner turmoil. "I'll hint to Baggard to follow up on the casino boss and see if a hit was placed on Sara. I doubt they'll get anywhere, but it's worth a shot."

I nodded, though my blood boiled over inside. My mind

kept returning to Pawsitive Academy and our visit there this morning. Something kept pulling my thoughts back to that place over and over again like a magnet. Though I couldn't put my finger on it, I was convinced the academy and Karen had played a role in Sara's death.

I was willing to bet that no one had put a hit out on the woman for the money she owed.

Now I just had to prove it.

CHAPTER NINETEEN

The fluorescent lights of the marquee flickered against the evening's hazy glow as I pushed open the heavy glass doors of the Gilded Clover Casino. A rush of sound hit me—spinning roulette wheels, clinking glasses, and the low hum of voices muffled beneath a constant whirring of whatever machines pumped air into this place.

The air carried the sharp tang of desperation and stale beer, mixing with the overpowering scent of lavender air freshener. It hit my sensitive vampire senses like a physical punch, and I barely kept from throwing up all over the dirty red carpet I stood on.

As I made my way further in, passing rows of slot machines that flashed promises of jackpots and dreams that would never materialize, I was shocked by how many people were there. The sticky residue on the carpet made it harder to get around, as though I was sinking into quick-sand. I briefly wondered if someone had designed the casino this way. To make sure people didn't leave.

A few heads turned my way as I passed, their expressions impossible to read. Probably on account of all the drinking. I ignored them, focusing instead on the task at hand.

I spotted the bar near the back, where amber pendant lights illuminated a man in a cowboy hat nursing a tumbler of something dark. His head was hunched over so deeply that I thought he might have drowned in the drink. A real class act.

Beyond the bar, a set of double doors led, presumably, to the office of the person I'd come to see. Mickey Sullivan. The man who'd supposedly taken out a hit on Sara. I planned to find out if that was the truth.

Ignoring the hoots and hollers from a group of men at a nearby poker table, I pulled open the doors.... and instantly plowed into a wall of muscle. Shoving away from the barreled chest I'd crashed into, I stared up at the man towering over me.

He was easily the size of Skeeter, if not taller. That was to say, he was gargantuan. Seriously, there was a shadow following him around that was so big it had painted the entire corridor a deep shade of black.

I gave him a sheepish smile. "Uh, hello there."

"Staff only beyond this point," he replied, voice gruff.

So much for sneaking in without being noticed. The entire

point of my not-so-covert operation was to get inside and do one of two things.

Best scenario side, I planned to charm my way into getting Mickey to tell me what I already knew: that he hadn't had anything to do with Sara's death.

And if things went south, I'd use my vamp abilities to get the truth out of him with compulsion. I hoped to avoid doing the latter, since it was a pain in the butt to recover from later and often left me with a raging headache that lasted for days. But it appeared I no longer had a choice on whether I used it.

I batted my eyelashes at the giant. Instantly feeling foolish, I dropped the act and looked up at the guard towering over me. My eyes locked on his and my magic sizzled through me. I knew the moment the connection formed because the giant's irises grew in size and his head slowly dropped forward.

"I'm here to see Mickey." I stretched on my tippy toes to place a hand on his shoulder. "He's expecting me. He said you should go take a lunch break."

There was a moment where I worried the compulsion hadn't worked and he'd toss me out by the scruff of my neck. It was the first time I'd tried to use my ability on someone so much larger than myself. Sweat beaded on my forehead and my toes curled inside my boots. There was a sudden heaviness in the air surrounding us.

The giant trembled, then flashed his yellow-stained teeth at me. "Of course. Last door on the left. Knock before you enter."

I breathed out a long-held breath. Skirting around the guard's wide figure, I scurried down the dimly lit corridor and toward the row of doors lining it. As I passed, I noted the number of locks on each one.

Most doors had clearly labeled brass plates on the wall next to them to signal what was inside. Security room. Janitor's closet. Break room. All were fairly standard for any business.

I walked by another door. This one differed from the rest. It was made of a thick metal and had five locks on it, not counting the one on the handle. My eyes narrowed on the fingerprint lock above all the others.

This must be the money vault.

Directly next to it stood an ornate wooden door without a label. This was it. Glancing back at the guard, I waved meekly, watching him walk out of the corridor and into the casino before I turned back to the boss's office door.

Raising my hand, I knocked on the wood three times.

"Who is it?" a muffled voice asked from within.

I thought about telling him the truth, but figured he'd call for his lackey the second he realized I had somehow snaked my way back here. Instead of answering, I steeled my spine and pushed open the door. As soon as the stuffy air from inside the office hit my nostrils, regret bloomed in my chest.

What the Van Helsing is wrong with me?!

Why had I thought barging in was a good idea?

For all I knew, the guy had a gun on him and from what I'd heard, Mickey wouldn't have hesitated to shoot an intruder. He definitely sounded like a trigger-happy type of fella who wasn't squeamish about things like blood and murder.

Cold sweat licked its way down my neck as the door swung open and bounced against the wall. Oops.

I stared at a short, stout man with an oversized toupee sitting behind a wide mahogany desk. His wiry brows shot upward as he inspected me standing in the doorway.

Mickey's swollen fingers spread on the table. "Who are you? How did you get in here?"

I eyed the man, more curious than scared. For the life of me, I could not understand why the mermaid was so afraid of the casino owner. Sure, he had a giant goon guarding his hiding hole, but for the most part, there was nothing intimidating about Mickey Sullivan.

Maybe I'm missing something...

Summoning every ounce of confidence I possessed, I gave him an easygoing smile and approached the desk.

When I was two feet from him, Mickey held up a hand. "That's close enough."

I tried my best not to snicker.

You're not scaring anyone, buddy.

"My name is Lyra." The lie rolled off my tongue. "I was a friend of Sara Cline. I believe you two were well acquainted?"

Before I could blink, Mickey had reached under his desk and, with a flick of his wrist, I found myself staring down the barrel of a gun. A second later, I heard the click of the door closing and locking behind me automatically.

I counted three distinct clicks as the bolts worked themselves into place. A hot lump formed in my throat as Mickey slowly cocked the trigger.

Okay, fine. Maybe he was a bit scary after all.

I opened my mouth to speak, but the casino owner cut me off.

"I'm going to ask you one more time, lady," Mickey said, his voice stern and serious. "Who are you, and how did you get inside?"

The beads of sweat on my neck rolled down my spine in cold droplets, and I shivered as they made their way beneath my sweater. Licking my dry lips, I focused on the gun pointing at me.

How had I ended up in this situation... again?

I really needed to stop placing myself in these life-or-death scenarios before someone got hurt. And by someone, I meant me.

Not making any sudden movements, I locked eyes with Mickey and said, "My name is Lia and I knew Sara Cline. As for how I got here"—I nudged my chin toward the door —"I just walked in. The door was unlocked."

"You expect me to believe that you strolled past Shep without so much as a blink of an eye?"

Shep. So that was the muscle at the door.

I scratched my head, acting as aloof as I could manage. "I'm not sure who that is, but there was no one here when I arrived."

"Hmm," the casino owner mused. The gun in his hand tipped slightly as his wrist relaxed. "So, Lia. What does

Cline want with me? If you're here to strike a deal, I'm not having it. You tell your friend she has two months to square up, or she's going to lose that house of hers. I don't do handouts. Not even for my wife's friends."

My wide eyes flicked to the sparkle of a gold around his ring finger. *Who in their right mind would marry this creepy guy?* I was appalled on the woman's behalf, and I didn't even know her.

Belatedly, my brain processed the rest of what he'd said.

Mickey Sullivan wanted me to relay information to Sara, and since you couldn't talk to the dead, it was quite clear that my original theory was correct. The casino owner had not killed her.

I crooked a questioning brow at him, trying to ignore the gun he'd shifted to point directly at my forehead. "Sara and your wife were friends?"

"Unfortunately. Hang on. Did you say 'were?'" Mickey asked, his eyes narrowing. "Why do you keep talking about Sara in the past tense?"

Uh oh. It was most definitely time to get out of here. My muscles twitched as I tapped into my vamp abilities, knowing Mickey wasn't going to let me leave before he got the answers to all his questions.

My head was already pounding from compelling the guard outside, but I didn't have another choice at the moment. I had already said too much, and I couldn't risk Mickey knowing that Sara was dead, at least not from me. As far as the casino owner was supposed to be concerned, I was never here. The last thing I needed was Officer Baggard getting wind of it.

I also didn't want Mickey to make good on the gun in his hand. It was either I use compulsion again or start praying that I was fast enough to dodge a bullet.

I still had trauma from grade-school dodgeball. If I wasn't fast enough to dodge those, I doubted I could outmaneuver a bullet, even with my vampiric speed.

Mickey's finger twitched on the trigger, but before he could pull it, I locked onto his mind and gathered every bit of energy I had left. It didn't take a lot to get a hold of Mickey's consciousness. For someone in the business he was in, the casino owner was shockingly easy to read.

His body relaxed, and he lowered the gun, resting it on the desk in front of him.

"I was never here," I spoke slowly, watching as Mickey nodded in agreement. "Shep is right outside the door and no one has stepped foot here in the last half hour."

He gave another nod, and I knew I had him completely hooked. I hated doing it to the poor guy, but it was me or him. And something told me that if the tables were reversed, Mickey wouldn't think twice about choosing his own well-being.

Leaving him to come out of the daze, I skulked out of the office, down the hall, and walked through the casino, my feet speeding up as I reached the front doors. The energy of the place was weighing me down, and I couldn't wait to put some distance between myself and the building.

The sound of slot machines dinged behind me, urging

me onward. As I walked, one thought repeated in my mind on a loop.

My theory was correct. Mickey hadn't killed her.

While I should've been happy, I was at a complete loss for words.

Things were not looking great for the case. And with Mickey off the suspect list, we were truly at a dead end.

CHAPTER TWENTY

The electric hum of the open refrigerator filled the kitchen of the clinic. I sat on the floor with my legs crossed, three empty Crimson Quench boxes lying at my feet. My mood had soured drastically since I'd left the casino, and even though I hadn't been scheduled to come in tonight, the thought of wallowing in self-pity at home gave me hives.

Instead, I headed to Sunny Days with the hope that burying myself in paperwork might have taken my mind off the fact that we were further from figuring out what happened to Dana and Sara than ever—which meant I was still a prime suspect as far as Officer Baggard was concerned; that didn't sit well with me at all.

I looked at the manila file folders splayed open before me and frowned. Thanks to my lack of focus, I'd managed to mix up several patient charts. Leafing through the papers, I took my time putting them back in the proper order.

At this rate, I'd be here all night doing more harm than good.

"How's it going, boss?"

I jumped and stared up to find Bree's smiling face watching me from the doorway. Her expression radiated happiness, sweeping away some of the gloom I was feeling.

Tonight, the pixie had styled her hair in a stunning array of countless delicate braids, each strand a different hue of the rainbow. She'd secured the braids into a cascading ponytail that bobbed and swayed as she walked toward me, keeping time with her every step like a metronome.

Beneath her white coat, a sparkly blue collar peeked out, a perfect match for her chosen eyeshadow in both color and vibrance. She had truly outdone herself today.

I returned her smile, though mine didn't quite reach my eyes.

"There's a good chance I mucked up the files." I looked at the stack to my right and grimaced. "Again."

"Wow. I've never seen you so down before. Are you really this stressed over the situation with that cop? What was his name? Bad breath?"

I chuckled. "Baggard," I corrected her. "And no, that's not what's bothering me."

Bree crossed the kitchen and slid down the wall to sit beside me. The aroma of cinnamon toast drifted off her as she reached over to close the refrigerator door, then settled her bright gaze on me.

"All right, let's hear it. What has got you mixing up charts and drowning your sorrows in blood juice boxes?"

I glanced at the door. "Shouldn't you be setting up for the clinic to open soon?"

The pixie waved me off.

"Grennich has it handled," she said. "Now spill."

"Ugh, fine," I sighed, dropping my head against the wall behind me. "I am certain Dana's and Sara's deaths are somehow connected, yet I can't prove it. Not only that, but so far, everything I'd come up with has led me to nothing but dead ends. And now I've gotten Ryder involved because of my stupid inability to let things go."

I paused to take a breath and steady the tremor in my voice. "Every day I seem to be digging myself into a deeper hole with the police. Plus, there's the whole fiasco with Benny, which has been keeping me up all hours of the day and night. Literally. Because someone tried to threaten me into giving up Ryder's dog, just so some oddball supernatural agency can do who knows what with the sweet hellhound."

Bree's eyebrows inched closer together, and she tilted her head to the side as if to see me better. She rested her hand on my shoulder, giving it a light squeeze.

"Wow, that is a lot. You weren't kidding," she said softly.

"I know. Maybe I should quit while I'm behind and let Baggard handle this."

"So he can pin it on you like he seems to want to do?" The pixie bristled like an angry hen.

I shrugged, all the fight gone from my body.

Bree's face soured as she took in my slumped shoulders. Her lips tightened into a line and her fierce expression sent a shiver down my spine.

She fixed me with a death glare. "Ophelia Pane! Since when do you give up?"

"Since I hit a wall."

"So what?" Bree scoffed. "How many walls did you hit when you set out to prove Ryder wrong after Justin died? I seem to recall you feeling much the same then. But you know what the difference was?"

"That Justin was my employee and sort of friend?"

"No!" Bree exclaimed, throwing up her hands in obvious exasperation. "The difference was that you kept going. And it wasn't because he was your vet tech. You knew things were off and you stuck to your gut."

"It's not the same," I groaned, my head suddenly too heavy to keep upright. "With Justin, I had plenty of hunches, and one of them happened to be the right one. But now it's as though my brain has stopped working. I actually had to compel two people in a row today because of how wrong I was. Two!"

"Ouch. Want some painkillers for your head?"

I waved her off. "I'll be fine. The blood boxes are helping."

Judging by the pity on Bree's face, the blood boxes were not, in fact, helping.

Why was this particular case getting me down? What

had happened to Justin was much closer to home, and yet it never affected me the way Dana's and Sara's death had.

Sure, I'd felt awful about what had happened and had been scared about being convicted of a crime I hadn't committed, but not once had I felt so helpless. What was it about now that made such a drastic difference?

I couldn't figure it out.

"Look here," Bree said, her words dragging me back to reality. "I don't want you to think I'm saying this because you're utterly miserable, but I really do believe you have a knack for these things."

I bristled. "What things?"

"This! Solving crimes. Finding information the police can't. Putting the puzzle together." She twirled her hand in the air. "Aside from being a vet, this is the only thing I've seen you do that made you happy, at least most of the time. Plus, you're helping people! Trust me when I tell you, the answer will come to you. I know it will."

Realization hit me.

The reason I was so upset over what was happening was because after the last case, I'd let myself believe I'd found something I was meant to do. I'd had the same epiphany when I realized I wanted to be a veterinarian. And then again when I'd decided to move to Bluejay Falls and open my own clinic.

Those choices had both been risks, but deep down, I'd felt I was on the right track to what I was always supposed to become.

And now I couldn't do it. I'd failed.

This time I couldn't replicate the magic and it was driving me out of my skin.

I was so caught up in my head that I didn't realize Bree had left the room. The kitchen was empty save for the muffled sounds of Grennich dragging chairs around in the waiting room and the dripping of the coffee machine the pixie must have turned on before stepping out.

My chest tightened.

Great, I'd driven her away with my over-dramatic melancholy. I stood up and picked up the file folders and empty Crimson Quench boxes to tidy up.

As I walked to the trash, a deep voice from the back door drew my attention. Blood pounded in my ears as I strained to hear.

Is that Ryder?

I poked my head through the doorway and peered down the passage. Surprise registered on my face at the sight of the detective chatting with Bree at the rear of the clinic. She leaned against the open door that led to the alley, her voice low and her brows tightly knit together.

What were those two talking about? And why was Ryder here?

I cleared my throat, making them both jump in surprise.

"Um, what's going on?" I asked.

Bree's lips tugged into a bright smile. "I called in backup." Then, turning to Ryder, she asked, "Did you bring it?"

"Sure did. Give me a minute."

"Bring what?" I asked, my interest piqued.

There was little time to get an answer because a second later, Ryder was back, and he had a large blackboard tucked under his arm. He wiggled his eyebrows, a mischievous glint in his green eyes.

Ryder winked at me. "Ready to work?"

"I-I don't understand," I stuttered.

It was true. I really had no clue what was happening.

Brushing past Bree, Ryder pointed to the board, saying, "Bree said you were stuck, so I offered to help you work the case. You should've told me you were feeling down, Lia. We're in this together, remember?"

I instantly felt foolish, although not as foolish as I'd feel if he found out about my trip to the casino.

Forcing a smile, I crossed my arms and stared at him. "Okay, but what's with the board?"

"Oh, we're going to do this the old school way," Ryder said. "We're making a detective board. Let's go."

Without waiting for me to reply, he strode past me and into my empty office. As Ryder started to set up his odd board of mystery, I turned my attention to Bree, who was all but bouncing on her toes. The pixie had done something good, and she knew it.

I made a mental note to get her a little something extra with her holiday gift and marched into the room after Ryder.

No more sulking, Lia Pane, I told myself.

It was time to figure out what had happened to Dana

and Sara. My vet tech was right—I did have a knack for these things, and I'd be staked if I didn't use it to solve the case.

CHAPTER TWENTY-ONE

"Don't forget the ex-husband," Ryder said as I balanced on my tippy toes on a chair, hovering over the blackboard.

I drew a line from the tacked photo of Dana to Lucas Jenkins, underlining his name twice. Stepping back, I inspected the board. It looked like a deranged version of a child's game—the kind you'd find on a disposable mat in a restaurant, with a million potential roads tangled in the shape of a maze.

Circles dotted the board like breadcrumbs, connected by a chaotic web of chalk in reds, blues, and blacks. Newspaper clippings, blurry photographs, and scribbled notes filled every available space, some overlapping in layers.

But only one road could lead to the right destination. The problem was, we had yet to find it. Instead, we continued to stare at a puzzle so dense it seemed at risk of collapsing under its own weight.

Like the puzzle, I'd also started to feel weighed down by the gravity of the situation. Staring at the board, it was easy to see why I was struggling to figure out a plausible theory to explain what had happened to both women.

At first glance, there was nothing in their lives that intersected except for how they knew each other. They spent time in different circles, lived at opposite ends of town, and led polar opposite personal lives.

I scratched the back of my head with a pen.

What tied them to one another? More importantly, what was the common denominator that had gotten them both killed?

I cocked my head to one side, hoping a fresh perspective might have offered some new ideas, then glanced over my shoulder at Ryder. The detective reclined against the low side table in the room, and I tried not to notice the veins running up his forearms when he lifted the sleeves of his sweater.

Averting my gaze, I focused on the board again, knowing I really didn't need any distractions... no matter how appealing it was. I still couldn't believe he was willing to spend his day off going over this case and working through the possibilities with me. He had no personal reason to be so involved in the case, so why was he being so helpful? Shouldn't he have been scolding me over getting involved in police matters?

"Lucas has no ties to Sara," I said grimly. "Neither does Dana's neighbor."

Ryder frowned. "And you're certain the neighbor is innocent?"

"Only as far as Dana's death is concerned. He was nowhere near the scene during the time she would've been killed," I said. "But I don't know what his whereabouts were when Sara fell."

"Allegedly fell," Ryder corrected.

I nodded. "Yes, right. Still, what reason would he have to hurt Sara? He didn't know her."

"That we can find so far. It's possible there is a connection between them we're not seeing." Ryder walked over to the board.

He bent toward the messy notes I had scribbled earlier, reading them intently. He picked up a Post-It note and walked to the opposite side of the board, comparing it to another set of notes.

The detective's eyes sparked with interest. "What about this lawsuit? Any validity to it, or was Sara blowing smoke to scare off the dog trainer?"

"I don't know," I said with a shrug. "I couldn't find any information on it. Which isn't surprising, if they had to keep it under wraps. But something has been bothering me about it ever since I found out there was a legal dispute between them."

"What's that?"

I pointed to the picture of Mickey Sullivan. "How did Sara afford a lawyer when she was in debt over her head?"

I thought back to Sara's lavish house. The wheels in my head started to spin uncontrollably. "Why would a woman who was so clearly well-off risk everything by gambling in the first place? You'd think she had enough money without needing more."

"Gambling is not always about making more money," Ryder said. "If she was in over her head, she may not have known how to stop."

"Why not pay Mickey off then? She clearly could afford it."

Ryder worked his jaw out, looking at me. "Unless she couldn't."

He held up a finger and reached into the back pocket of his jeans to pull out his cell phone. Scrolling through his contacts, he clicked on a name and waited for the line to ring, his eyes never leaving mine.

When whoever he called finally picked up, Ryder cleared his throat, saying, "Hey, Trev. I need a favor. You know that case Baggard caught... Yeah, the woman who fell down the stairs. Any chance you can forward me the file? Specifically, anything he had on her financials."

There was a long pause, and Ryder nodded while the other person spoke.

"Yeah, I know. He's gunning for the wrong person," Ryder said when it was his turn to speak. "I don't want him knowing I'm going over his head, so if you could keep this on the down low, I'd appreciate it."

Another pause came that had my anxiety skyrocketing.

"Thanks," Ryder said when his friend agreed. "I owe you one."

When he hung up and put his phone away, I asked, "Now what?"

"Now we wait," he said. "I'm going to put on a pot of coffee. Do you want anything from the kitchen?"

I shook my head and watched him walk out of the room. Turning back to the board, I reread everything we'd compiled, going over the information with a fine-toothed comb. There was something here we were missing, I was certain of it. A connection that was so obvious that we'd probably over-looked it by concentrating on the more intricate pieces.

What was it that my dad always said? Go easy or go home. Sure, he mostly meant it as an excuse to speed clean when my mom nagged him about the state of his office, but the gist was the same. The easiest and fastest route was often the smartest one to choose.

I read through the timeline once more, ignoring all the added fluff that didn't have anything to do with the deaths directly.

Sara hires Dana to train her poodle.

She fires her after a disagreement on methods used.

My eyes narrowed on the word 'lawsuit' and the under-lined question mark following it.

Sara leaves the dog trainer and possibly sues her.

The following year, Dana was seen arguing with her ex-husband shortly before she was found dead in the dog park.

Fast forward to a week after Dana's death, and Sara accidentally tripped down her basement stairs.

I stopped reading. Picking up the white chalk from the tray under the board, I added the note, *'Sara receives a mysterious call before she died,'* then stepped back.

Could that be what had bothered me about the board? Was the call important? It didn't seem to be from the way Sara had acted, but maybe there was something there we should have followed up on. I made a mental note to check with Ryder, then returned my attention to the information we did have.

Which, in all honesty, didn't amount to much.

"I got it," Ryder declared, walking back inside.

He waved his phone in the air, a steaming cup of coffee balanced in his other hand.

"Your friend on the force sent Sara's bank records?"

He gave a short nod. "He sure did. I can always count on Trev to come through. We trained for the job together, so we go back a long way."

I smiled, sitting down in a chair. "What's the deal with the records?"

"They're kind of strange, actually." Ryder flicked through the message from his friend, his expression darkening. "It's as I suspected. Sara Cline was only wealthy in appearances."

My eyebrows rose. "She was broke?"

"Only as of last year," Ryder said. "According to this, she made large, back-to-back donations to several charities. Enough to put her in the red."

"Why would she do that? It doesn't make sense."

The thing that kept nagging at the back of my brain was back.

I glanced at Ryder. "What type of charities?"

"Looks to be all animal rights places," he replied. "A few other humanitarian organizations, but the majority all have something to do with protecting animals from abuse."

There was a small part of me that fought to focus on the information Ryder was reading off, but my mind became fixated on the new thought that barged into my head. I stared at the board, my heart racing in my chest as I realized there was another piece of evidence we'd forgotten to add to the board.

"Hold that thought," I told Ryder.

Using the chalk, I moved to the area of the board detailing Dana's death and added a quick note beneath the location.

"The smell," I murmured. "There was a garlic smell in the dog park when I found Dana."

"Um… all right. And that's relevant how?" Ryder asked, confused.

Memories of my visit to Pawsitive Academy flashed before me, and my mind raced as I started fitting the pieces together. The garlic smell. The assortment of posters tacked to the wall.

My eyes widened, remembering a flyer for an animal abuse rally happening this coming weekend.

Another image swam before me, and my blood cooled.

I spun around to face Ryder. "The lip balms," I whispered.

"The what now?"

I waved him off. *Holy bat wings!*

My gaze jumped between the board and the detective as a rush of clarity and exhilaration raced through my body. It was as though the fog of uncertainty had lifted and everything was clicking into place. A thrill danced through me.

"I know who it is," I gasped. "I know who killed Dana and Sara!"

CHAPTER TWENTY-TWO

R yder insisted on driving, and I didn't bother about arguing. Normally, I'd want to be behind the wheel, but right then, all I wanted was to stare blankly out the window as the trees blurred outside. The sun had set hours ago, and the sky was the shade of a blooming bruise—dark and unforgiving.

I rubbed the ridge of my nose in exasperation. "I can't believe I didn't see it before."

"Don't be too hard on yourself," Ryder said, turning off the main road and onto a wild path. "She fooled me too."

The second I'd recalled the lip balms at Pawsitive Academy, the same brand as Dana's, things clicked into place. The strange garlic smell at the dog park the night I'd found her had grated on me since, but I could never pinpoint why. Now it all made sense. Other than delicious foods, there was one more thing that could leave a lingering scent so foul.

Arsenic.

Someone had poisoned Dana with arsenic. It couldn't have been a large dose, or else it would have been too obvious. The symptoms would have been too clear. No, they had to do it in slow doses.

Shivers trailed down my spine.

Slow dosing arsenic could have multiple side effects, but one of the more pronounced ones was the paralysis. I recalled it from vet school when we studied various types of poisoning in household pets.

If Dana was paralyzed, it would have been easy enough to make it appear as though she'd choked. The poor woman wouldn't have been able to fight back.

I thought back to finding the body in the dead of night, with Benny growling at my side. The murder weapon had been right there, and no one had thought to check because all signs pointed to an accident.

Now it was clear as day as we drove down the winding paths between the trees.

The lip balm. The arsenic was in her lip balm.

The same lip balm she'd gotten from the Pawsitive Academy's supply. A gift from Karen, I'd have bet.

"How could someone who cares so much about personal well-being, of people and their dogs, kill a person over a business rivalry?" I asked Ryder.

The detective's fingers tensed on the wheel. "People have killed for less." He took another sharp turn toward the academy.

"It would make sense, though. If Karen killed Dana and Sara figured it out, she'd likely want to get rid of her, too. It fits." I pointed out.

"Only one way to find out," Ryder said as he pulled the car into the driveway to park. "Remember, we are only here to scope out more evidence and confirm our suspicions. We can't use anything we discover here, so we'll need to figure out another way to bring this information to Baggard."

I nodded. "Got it. In and out. I promise."

The academy loomed in front of us. Set against the night sky and hovering over us, it seemed like a gloomy sentinel of dark secrets. Unlike the first two times I'd visited, seeing the log cabin at night definitely gave it horror vibes rather than that of a charming resort getaway. The glossy wood walls glimmered in the moonlight and the darkened windows made the place appear more sinister than the peaceful grounds I had recalled from before.

Even the training grounds beyond the main building seemed to resemble a torture chamber of crooked structures that screamed for a much-needed escape.

I sat up straight and bit my lip. "How do we get inside?"

"I was hoping you could help with that," he said.

When he pointed to the chimney on the cabin's roof, I nearly fainted.

No fangin' way!

The detective didn't expect me to bat myself into that thing, did he? Surely that was not his idea.

"Think you can fly up there and turn the alarm off from the inside?"

Oh. He did it. Stab me with a stake and call me a shish kabob!

I groaned, and despite my misgivings, I begrudgingly agreed to his ridiculous plan. As much as I didn't want to use my abilities in front of Ryder, he wasn't wrong. It was the only way we could get into the academy without being detected. And since he wasn't here on official police business, I doubted he wished to be caught red-handed breaking down doors. I didn't know how the police force worked, but I was fairly certain there would be reprimands for that. If not worse.

Yep. I needed to make sure Ryder didn't get in trouble for trying to help me out of a tight spot. Instructing him to stay on watch at the front, I looped around the rear of the house and glanced around. Once I was sure I was alone and Ryder hadn't followed me, I stripped down, closed my eyes, and called forth the transformation.

In a flash, my human body evaporated, and I was flying sky high, backlit by the glow of the moon. Taking a deep breath, I descended into the chimney. As I dropped into the inky darkness, I thanked my lucky stars no one used the contraption. At least I wouldn't be coating my lungs in smoky soot just to gain access to the stupid academy.

Pale light appeared below me, and I eagerly flapped toward it, shooting out of the fireplace and into the front waiting room. Moving quickly, I shifted forms and scanned the area for something to cover myself up with.

The thought of Ryder seeing me in my birthday suit made my brain short circuit temporarily. I shook myself back to reality, my gaze darting frantically around the dim area for a solution. My eyes landed on a hook near the door and relief flooded my body.

Hanging by the door was what appeared to be a padded full-body suit. I wasn't sure why the academy would need one—perhaps for extra aggressive dogs—but I didn't really care. The suit would surely cover me from head to toe, and though movement might have been difficult, it beat the alternative… which was showing the detective a lot more of me than was necessary.

I padded toward the suit, slipping into it and zipping it up as high as it would go. Sweat slicked my skin as soon as I was bundled up. The darn thing was hotter than an oven, and despite the cold weather, I was regretting the decision to wear it. I wiped my wet brow and headed for the door.

Dread filled me as I stopped in front of the security code box, eyeing it suspiciously.

"Ryder? Are you there?" I whisper-shouted.

The soft thud of his boots was followed by the sound of the detective cursing as he tripped over something on the front porch.

"Here," he growled a moment later. "Can you get it open?"

"I'm not sure. I think I need a code to disarm the door alarm." My eyes darted around the waiting room. "Let me see if I can find it written down somewhere."

The light of an emergency exit sign above the door

helped illuminate some of the space, casting shadows on the rows of chairs near one wall. I moved cautiously, careful not to trip over anything as I searched. Scurrying to the reception desk, my fingers brushed over the smooth surface as I felt for anything at all—a piece of paper, a notebook, anything to give me a clue as to where a code might be written down.

Skirting around the desk, I crouched low, my breath shallow as I strained to check in the drawers below. It was too dark to make anything out clearly. I didn't want to risk turning on my phone's flashlight in case someone happened to be driving by. It was doubtful anyone would be here at this hour, but knowing my luck, it was better to be safe than sorry.

I found that the first drawer I tried was unlocked. Inside, there were file folders with client information and several hand-written notebooks about new dog training techniques. It was nearly impossible to make out the words, but if I squinted, I could get the gist of what was written down. Nothing that looked like a code for the alarm.

I pushed aside a stack of papers, pausing as an envelope tumbled out. The name on the front caught my eye, and a breath got trapped in my throat as I picked up the envelope to see what was inside.

"Dana Seller," I read the name out-loud.

What was an envelope addressed to Dana doing in the academy? Hands trembling, I opened it and looked inside. The contents were sparse, but as I read the first few sentences of the letter, my heart dropped to my feet.

It was a work contract.

I struggled to breathe, my paper-thin lungs refusing to expand. Karen had hired Dana to work as a trainer at the academy two weeks before she'd died.

It didn't make any sense.

Why would Karen kill her if she'd just taken her on as an employee?

My body vibrated.

I stood up with the contract clutched in my sweaty fingers and headed for the door. "Hey, Ryder—"

A distant metallic clang had me frozen in my tracks. The sound came from somewhere in the building... somewhere close by. Had Ryder found another way to get inside?

I turned around, the heaviness of the suit I wore making the air ripple around me. A smell drifted toward me and my nose twitched as it swirled into my nostrils.

Patchouli.

The familiarity of it brought back the last memory I had the first time I'd stood in this same waiting room. It was odd because it wasn't there when Ryder and I had returned to question Karen, so wherever the smell came from, it wasn't a permanent fixture at the academy.

The breath caught in my lungs.

Hadn't Baggard said something about being allergic to incense when he'd had the sneezing fit in Sara's home? I'd assumed that Sara enjoyed burning it, but now...

Shock spurred me into action and I rushed for the chimney to make my escape, but something hard smacked into the back of my head.

My vision blurred, black dots swirling in the air surrounding me. Head foggy, I stumbled, hitting the side of the desk with a loud thud. With my balance faltering, I clumsily dropped to the floor on my knees. Pressing a hand to my head, I pulled it away, a fresh wave of terror racing through me when I noticed it was wet and sticky.

Before me, a dark, looming figure approached.

I wasn't alone anymore, and that wasn't Ryder.

The smell of patchouli continued to swirl around me as my vision bled to black. As the darkness took over, my last thought was of how wrong I'd been.

Karen wasn't the killer.

The real killer was right in front of me.

CHAPTER TWENTY-THREE

T he room spun as I fought to open my eyes. Had someone glued my eyelids together?

There was a chill in the air that seeped into my bones and my head throbbed something fierce. Every molecule in my body begged for us to go back to sleep. I groaned, the sound muffled through the fog in my brain.

When I finally managed to open my eyes, the world looked like a kaleidoscope of fractured pieces, like shards of broken glass. A dull, throbbing ache pulsed at the base of my skull, radiating outward with each sluggish heartbeat. My thoughts were thick and muddled and I struggled to connect them. It was as though I was trying to force a key into the wrong lock.

Wait... lock.

I'd been looking for a way to unlock something before this, hadn't I?

There was a biting cold at my wrists that made my awareness sharpen. I blinked, desperately trying to clear my vision and, to my horror, I discovered the cause. Metal shackles were clamped tightly around my wrists, my arms stretched and pinned awkwardly above my head.

I squinted at the shackles, realizing they weren't shackles at all.

Who the heck had chained me to a wall with a dog leash?

I tried to shift my weight, but the chains rattled in protest, sending sharp pains up my arms. Panic flared within me and adrenaline curved up my spine. Still fighting the sleep that tried to drag me under, I forced myself to take in my surroundings. I was in some sort of room—probably a basement, I guessed, on account of there not being any windows.

Breath coming in fast pants, I tested the restraints again, pulling harder this time. The chains held fast and the throbbing in my skull intensified.

A shuffling sound drew my attention to the opposite side of the room. I gasped. Ryder was down here too, and he wasn't fairing much better. Actually, judging by the blood dripping down his forehead and staining his jacket, he seemed to be in worse shape.

"Ryder," I whispered. Then, when he didn't respond, I hissed louder, "Ryder!"

He came to slowly, his eyes hazy and unfocused. "Lia? What happened?"

I bit the inside of my cheek, my memories slowly returning to me.

How could I have missed it? Now that I knew what had happened, the obviousness of the truth seemed to be laughing at me. I ground my teeth together.

"It was Casey," I said.

Ryder's body grew taut. "The academy owner's niece? Why?"

"Actually, I'm not entirely sure why," I admitted. "But it's her. I know it."

"Well, whatever the reason, it doesn't matter right now," Ryder said. "We have got to get out of here before she comes back." He yanked hard on the chains holding him down in place. "And she took my gun. Great."

I studied the metal around his wrists. "Can you shift?"

"To wolf form?" Ryder thought about it, testing the restraints again. He sighed and his shoulders slumped. "Probably not in this position. She has me pinned pretty good, and I doubt my wolf form could get out of these without breaking some bones."

"Good point. Let's try to avoid that."

The low light had started to lift as my eyes adjusted to the conditions of the room we were in. I scanned the room to see what we could use to free ourselves as soon as possible. Ryder was right; we needed to get a move on if we were going to escape before Casey returned. My eyes narrowed on every object in the room.

Across from me, stacks of large posters leaned against the wall, their edges curling. The top one featured a snarling dog behind bars with bold letters that read *Stop the Torture!* above its furry face. Nearby, a heap of spray-paint cans sat beside a half-empty box of crumpled pamphlets detailing protests against animal cruelty. There were several crates that appeared to be out of use and a table with folded chairs leaning against it. Near to those, a rickety old staircase led to the upper level of the building with a door I was certain was locked from the outside.

I scanned the room for something—anything—I could use. There was an overturned mop bucket and a cracked plastic toolbox half-buried under a tangle of extension cords. A pair of bolt cutters peeked out from under a filthy blanket in the far corner, but they were too far out of reach. My pulse quickened as I thought of the possibilities.

"See anything useful?" Ryder whispered.

"Maybe," I muttered, eyes darting toward the paint can opener a few feet away.

If I could only get to it. A noise from up the stairs made me freeze.

"Keep quiet," I warned Ryder.

Above us, faint footsteps echoed. I tugged again at the chain leash, the buckle rattling against the wall. *If I can loosen it a bit more, I might be able to reach the metal handle.* My heart thundered against my ribcage as I leaned forward, every creak of the leash threatening to alert our captor to the fact that I was awake.

There was no telling what Casey had planned, but she'd probably get down here pretty quickly if she knew we were trying to escape.

Straining, I stretched out my leg and kicked at the pile of papers sitting beside the can opener. Swinging it from side to side, I worked to get momentum to kick the papers over so I could reach at least one of them.

After several attempts, I finally turned over the pile, sending the leaflets flying all over the floor. I caught glimpses of the contents as they fluttered down. More animal activism flyers. These appeared to be from a march last week and were sponsored by the academy and a company called the Sanctuary Society. There were logos for the group all over the flyers.

Why did that name sound so familiar?

I stopped flailing to turn to Ryder. "Do you remember the name of the company Sara invested her money in?"

"Sanctuary something-or-other," he said.

"Sanctuary Society," I confirmed. "The same place that sponsored all these rallies and marches."

Ryder's eyes turned to slits. "That's a strange coincidence."

"I don't believe it is a coincidence."

Once more, I stretched out my leg until it felt like it might pop out of its socket and slammed my foot down on top of one loose flyer, dragging it closer to me. Then I thrust my leg sideways, sliding the flyer across the floor like a magician yanking away a table cloth without breaking any plates. The paper slipped under the paint can opener.

Inch by painfully slow inch, I dragged the paper, and by extension the can opener, closer. "Here goes nothing," I muttered.

Right as I gripped the opener with my feet, the door to the basement burst open. My gaze shot up to the figure in the doorway. Casey stood silhouetted in the blinding light spilling in from upstairs.

She regarded the makeshift key between my feet with a sneer. Wisps of golden-blonde hair framed her face and there was a sharp glint in her pale, cold eyes. Her lips curved into a faint smile as she took the stairs one by one, reaching the bottom landing slowly.

There was something unnerving about her movements, as if she knew something we didn't. Dressed in a fitted coat that clung to her thin frame, she looked fragile at first glance—but I knew better. She'd managed to subdue me in seconds, not to mention taking Ryder out.

The smell of patchouli wafted into the basement as Casey stepped into the cramped space. The annoying grin on her face widened when she approached me, her foot kicking at mine and knocking the can opener away from me.

"It won't do you any good," she said casually. "The leashes are made to hold dogs much stronger than you."

I shot a look at Ryder from the corner of my eye. Little did she know there was someone a heck of a lot stronger than one of her dogs in here. I watched Ryder quietly work to free himself.

If only I could buy him some time, perhaps he could slip out of the leash and get a hold of Casey. At this point, I didn't care if he wolfed out on her as long as I got out of these stupid cuffs.

I glared at Casey. "Why did you do it?"

"You're joking, right?" she countered. Her arms spread wide, and she twirled around the length of the basement, gesturing to the flyers and posters overtaking the tight space. "This is my entire life. Helping poor innocent animals that can't help themselves. And if I get rich while doing it, I don't see the harm. Look how much good I'm doing!"

"But Dana wasn't hurting animals," I said. "She was a dog trainer. Like your aunt."

Casey scoffed. "That horrible woman was nothing like my aunt. She was cruel, and her pathetic excuse for training was borderline abusive. I mean, look what she did to Roxie!"

"Honestly, Roxie seemed fine to me when I met her…"

"Then you don't understand anything," Casey seethed. "The second I heard my aunt was hiring that monster, I knew I had to take matters into my own hands. She would destroy everything we built here. Everything!"

My gaze instinctively darted to Ryder, who gave me a quick nod, confirming that he was of the same mindset as I was.

Casey was completely off her rocker. Heck, I wasn't sure she even possessed a rocker at this point.

It was one thing not to like Dana or to have issues with how she trained her dogs, but to go so far as to kill her was —well, as she herself put it—monstrous.

My brow furrowed. "Couldn't you have simply asked Karen not to hire her?"

"I did!" she screeched. "My aunt wouldn't hear of it. She said Dana came with a big client list and we needed the money. That was all she cared about, anyway. She even dropped out of backing Sanctuary Society."

"Your aunt funded your activist group?"

Casey nodded, her nose flaring. "She used to. Until Dana convinced her she'd be better off putting that money into expanding the business and encouraged her to hire someone to help oversee my accounts. Dana had to go before she caused me any more problems."

Flashes of my conversation with Ryder prior to coming here played out in my head. I stared at Casey in disbelief, my mouth going dry. The lump in my throat grew in size and I tried to swallow it down, but it wouldn't budge.

I couldn't believe what I was hearing. For someone who had such deep passion when it came to saving animals, Casey was heartless.

"That was why you convinced Sara to invest in the group," I stated. When she nodded, I added, "And she found out what you did to Dana, didn't she? And then what? Did she threaten to turn you in to the police?"

"Worse," Casey said. "She wanted to pull out her investments, too. All I worked for would be ruined! I couldn't let her do that. Not after everything I'd done to make a difference in the world."

"So you killed her over it?"

"What? No!" Casey yelped. "I tried to talk her out of it. To tell her that her contributions were important, that what we were doing was important. But she didn't care. She kept talking about Dana and what happened and then…" Casey shrugged. "I guess she missed a step and fell down. I got out of there as fast as I could."

I snorted, unconvinced. "What about the phone call Sara received while she was jogging? That was you, wasn't it?"

A darkness settled over Casey's expression, and a muscle ticked in her jaw. "How did you know about that?"

I didn't need to hear more to know she was lying. Casey had killed Sara, and she'd gone there with every intention of doing so.

She'd lured her back into her home while she was there, waiting to make her move. Everything Casey had done was to save her own neck and make sure the work she was so proud of could continue and her bank account would keep growing. It seemed liked she'd done a lot of good with her group, but that was no excuse. Two people were dead and neither of them had deserved it.

Casey had to pay for what she did.

"What's your plan here?" I asked.

I was genuinely interested, since there was no getting out of this for her. The woman had killed two people and was holding a police detective against his will in a basement—one did not walk or talk their way out of this no matter how she tried to spin it.

Instead of answering, she walked over to the table and pulled open a drawer. She reached into it, her eyes darting between me and Ryder the entire time.

When she pulled out her hand, the blood in my veins turned to ice water.

I stared at the gun she pointed at me, blinking rapidly. "Casey, you don't want to—"

She clicked off the safety, lifting her arm as she walked toward me. From her angle, she was planning on shooting me right through the heart. I swallowed, licking my chapped bottom lip.

I could probably survive it as long as I didn't bleed out, but it was going to hurt like a son-of-a-biscuit-eater!

"I wish it didn't have to be this way," Casey said conversationally.

The crazed look in her eyes made them appear glazed over. As her finger tightened on the trigger, my mind went blank, and I squeezed my eyelids shut. They said that our lives flashed before our eyes when you were about to die, and yet I didn't feel anything of the sort. There was simply nothing.

Just me and the seconds ticking away before the bullet reached my chest.

A loud thud had my eyelids flying open, and I stared in wide-eyed shock at Casey's limp form on the ground. The gun was still in her hands, but she was completely out of it. Behind her, a massive wolf snarled, its teeth snapping.

The wolf's thick, silver-gray fur rippled across its broad shoulders as it moved around Casey's figure, stalking closer to me. Predatory green eyes locked onto me causing my entire body to tremble.

I'd treated enough wolves to know I was going to be in trouble if Ryder lost control of his wolf and forgot his humanity.

"Easy, Ryder," I pleaded, keeping my voice calm.

The wolf stopped in its tracks, tilting its head to study me.

Relief flooded my system as Ryder started to shift back to human form. I clamped my eyes closed to give him some privacy. It was the least I could do after he'd saved my life.

While I waited for him to get dressed in what was left of his clothes after his unexpected shift, I couldn't help but replay the events of the night. I was lucky Ryder was here. Had I gone through with my plan to investigate on my own, as I often tended to do, things could have ended far differently.

If I was going to be putting myself in drastic situations, I needed to get better at using my abilities. No more shying away from who and what I was.

CHAPTER TWENTY-FOUR

The detective had, in fact, broken a few bones while shifting and getting out of the restraints that had bound him. After he freed me, I called the police station, making sure they sent Officer Baggard to the academy to pick up the real killer he was searching for.

Archie wasn't exactly pleased to be wrong, and he was even less impressed by having to thank me for bringing Casey to justice. To his credit, he did offer me a mumbled apology.

After Casey came to and admitted to everything she did, while being cuffed, there was no denying I had nothing to do with either murder.

Watching Officer Baggard scowl at me as he climbed into his cruiser was the cherry on the cake. It was one less thing I had to worry about for now, though I doubted Archie would become my number one fan anytime soon.

I helped Ryder into an ambulance and drove his car down to his apartment building so it would be there when he got released. According to the doctors, he would be fine as long as he took it easy for a while and didn't try to scratch under the cast on his arm. I didn't have the heart to tell the physician that asking a werewolf to resist scratching an itch was the equivalent of asking a fish to stay out of the water.

Over the next few weeks, things seemed to go back to normal, or as normal as they could be, all things considered. The clinic was busier than usual, but with Grennich around, we were managing it well. I'd even been able to take several days off to mentally and physically recover—which I spent watching movies with Byrd and dodging calls from my mother.

Casey's case had somehow made its way into the national news, and my face, alongside Ryder's, had been plastered all over online blogs and papers. The worst part of it all was the cheesy headlines.

"Local Vet Saves More Than Your Loving Pets!"

"A Veterinarian and Detective Team Up to Solve Crimes!"

And my personal favorite: *"Vet by Day, Heroic Vigilante by Night!"*

The entire thing was utterly foolish, but it had gone straight to my mother's head and she wouldn't stop badgering me with questions about who Ryder was and why I was taking my sweet time sinking my fangs into him.

It was enough to make me consider canceling my cell

phone plan. Worse, she was threatening to come visit. There were many things I could survive, but a matchmaking visit from my mother was not one of them.

I shuddered, pulling up the blanket I nestled under up to my chin.

"What are we watching next, Byrd?" I asked.

The bat opened one lazy eye to peer at me from his side of the couch, then fell back asleep.

"Fine. I'll choose." I picked up the remote. "But no complaints if it's a movie you hate."

As I clicked through the menu, the doorbell rang, startling Byrd and causing me to jump. The bat chittered angrily and scooted under the blanket until only half his little face was visible. He glared at the front door with hatred.

"I wonder who that could be?" I asked Byrd, receiving no response. Obviously.

Grudgingly, I unrolled myself from the pretzel position I was in and stood up, making my way to the door. Rising on my tiptoes, I peered through the peephole.

I let out a gasp of surprise, unlocked the latch, and swung the door wide open to smile up at the werewolf detective standing on my porch.

"Ryder! This is a surprise," I said gleefully. "Did we have plans I forgot about?"

Ryder shook his head. "No, no. I'm really sorry to interrupt your day off."

"Totally fine." My chest warmed in delight, and realizing I was a little too eager to see him, I quickly shoved that feeling to the back of my mind. "I was just about to put a movie on. Want to join me?"

"On any other day, yes. But I'm afraid this isn't a regular visit."

Before I could understand what was happening, a ball of energy darted between my legs. Slick, snowy paws tapped at my knees as Benny destroyed my last good pair of jogging pants with his utter excitement.

Unable to resist his cuteness, I giggled, bending down to pet the puppy. "Hello to you too, Benny."

"What are we? Chopped liver?"

My neck strained to lean around Ryder's wide chest. I followed the familiar voice to find Bree and Grennich standing behind him, each armed with a giant Tupperware box.

"What's going on?" I asked suspiciously.

Bree and Grennich exchanged furtive glances behind the detective's back. As my attention dropped to the boxes they held, I slowly realized what they were carrying and my eyes widened.

"Are those Grennich's spell supplies?" I asked.

"Sure are!" the healer fae answered cheerfully.

I stepped aside, letting Bree and Grennich bustle inside, before turning to face Ryder again. "So... what's this about?"

The detective shrugged and walked into my house. "Grennich thinks she knows how to camouflage Benny. It won't be a permanent solution, but at least it will buy me enough time to figure out how to handle the situation with the SJD."

"That's great news!" I exclaimed. "Whatever it is, it's worth a shot." Closing the front door, I turned to the fae. "What do you need us to do?"

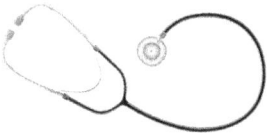

Two hours later, my kitchen looked and smelled like a pack of werewolves had held their full moon party in there. After everything that had happened, I'd had more than my fair share of scents, but I couldn't stop Grennich from taking over with her spells and potions—not when Benny's safety was on the line. So instead of complaining, I plugged my nose and did as I was instructed.

The entire point of them coming here, other than to include me, was to distract Benny with Byrd's presence. Since the spell Grennich had discovered needed time to steep and even more time to penetrate Benny's essence, we needed the dog to cooperate and not fight Grennich's magic with his own. And chasing after Byrd was a wonderful way to make him think about anything other than the spell working on him.

I watched the fae douse Bree in some sort of liquid that glowed immediately upon contact with her skin.

"You really think you can use Bree's pixie magic to change Benny's magical signature?" I asked. "Wouldn't he still look like himself?"

Grennich wiggled her brows, pouring more of the liquid on Bree's arms. "That's the best part," she said. "Because pixies have the ability to alter their appearance, we can borrow it and use it to change Benny's as well."

"That's actually..." I paused. "Brilliant. So Benny will still be Benny, but to everyone else, he will look like—"

"A fluffy, chubby tabby cat!" Bree squealed excitedly.

I laughed, picturing it... only to wince as a loud clamor came down the hallway.

"How long until it takes hold?" I asked. "I'm afraid I won't have a house left if we leave those two to their shenanigans for much longer."

On cue, a black blur flapped into the kitchen as Byrd darted past us and toward the cabinets. He landed on the highest available perch, chittering at an incoming Benny the entire time. A second later, the puppy came tumbling out of the hallway, his nose up in the air in search of his favorite winged companion.

Except Benny wasn't a puppy anymore...

I gasped. "No way! It worked!"

The four of us stared in disbelief as a large cat waddled between our legs. Its fluffy tail wagged back and forth, and it panted when it spotted Byrd's hiding spot. The cat, or Benny, tried to jump onto the counter, but its front legs only slid across the cabinet doors and landed on the ground. Frustrated, he tried again, with much the same result.

"I take it he didn't inherit a cat's agility, only its looks?" Ryder joked.

Bree shook her head. "The cat form is only an illusion. Kind of like my hair," she pointed to the iridescent gold strands on her head. "He is still very much a dog."

From the corner of the kitchen, Benny whined.

"A dog that needs a walk... badly," Ryder said. "I'll go take him out. Want to join, Lia?"

I smiled and scooped Benny up into my arms, snuggling him close as I walked after Ryder toward the front door. It was difficult to avoid the knowing glares of my co-workers —er, friends—as we passed. And it was even more difficult when they started snickering behind our backs like school-girls. I shot them both a death stare and rolled my eyes as Ryder draped my coat over my shoulders.

A gust of winter wind blasted my face as soon as we stepped outside. It was so cold out now that I doubted we'd be able to stay out for long without turning into ice sculptures. Still, it was nice to get some fresh air, especially since the smell in the kitchen was making my head spin.

The snow crunched beneath my boots as I walked down the street next to Ryder, the sunlight spilling like liquid gold across the frosted world. It wasn't the biting cold that made me snuggle deeper into my coat. No, it was more the nerves that foolishly weaved their way through my mind and heart.

The air was crisp, sharp in that invigorating way only winter could manage where the town came alive with details and the soft flutters of snowflakes that landed in my hair. It was my favorite part of the year because the town looked like something out of a postcard: cobblestone streets dusted with snow, wreaths on every door, and all the sounds of people rushing about their days.

It was simply magical.

A few people smiled as we passed, but their grins quickly faded when their eyes met Benny.

I laughed, nudging Ryder in the ribs. "We must look like a hot mess walking a cat on a leash in the middle of winter."

"It's going to take some getting used to, that's for certain," he agreed with a rumbling laugh.

We traipsed in comfortable silence for several more blocks, and I couldn't help but smile the entire time. It was nice to do something so mundane after the high-stress weeks we'd experienced lately. Every few steps, I'd catch a glimpse of the cast on Ryder's arm, and my smile would falter.

I couldn't believe the extent the detective had gone through to save me that night. I mean, sure, he'd sworn to protect the citizens of Bluejay Falls, but breaking your arm to shift while chained to the floor was really going above and beyond the call of duty.

It made me like him all the more for it.

"You haven't seen anyone lurking around your house recently, have you?" Ryder asked. "After the break in to warn you about Benny, that is."

And there it was. The real reason Ryder had asked me to join him on the walk.

We never did figure out who'd gotten a whiff of Benny's hellhound heritage and broken into my home to threaten us. With everything that had happened, I'd almost forgotten about the entire fiasco. Or maybe I'd chosen not to think about it because the idea of someone coming into my house uninvited made me itchy.

I frowned, looking up at the detective. "Nothing out of the ordinary," I answered. "We're probably safe for a while. Hopefully, whoever it was will think we gave Benny up and leave us alone."

We watched in silence as Benny-cat raised his back leg to pee on a tree trunk.

I snickered. "Although we should probably keep an eye out and keep him out of sight as much as possible. At least for a while."

"Agreed." The detective pressed his lips together, then blew out a long breath. "Please tell me if you see anything at all. I hate that I put you in danger. It was the last thing I intended."

I lightly tapped on his cast. "I know. And thank you again for saving me. It was pretty heroic."

"That's me," Ryder said with a chuckle. "Your wolf in shining armor."

He rubbed the back of his neck, his skin flushing. The detective's step slowed down while we waited for Benny to stop sniffing a random spot on the pavement.

Ryder's eyes found mine, and every molecule in my body started to vibrate at what I saw there.

"Do you think you'd want to go out to dinner with me sometime?" Ryder asked.

"Detective Wolff, are you asking me out on a date?" I teased.

"Trying to," Ryder replied, his gaze sliding away from mine as though he feared I would say no.

"In that case, yes," I said. "I'd love to go out to dinner with you."

A ball of fur bounded straight into my legs as Benny-cat body checked me so hard I stumbled backward. My boots caught on something on the ground and I toppled back, my balance giving out on me in a flash.

Ryder reached out his good arm to catch me, but the leash in his hand tangled with my fingers and I ended up pulling him down with me. We crashed into the large snow-bank on the side of the street, fluffy snow exploding around us like confetti.

A moment later, Benny-cat did a flying swan dive into the bank as well. He landed on top of us, his tongue lolling out as he panted with excitement.

Laughter bubbled from me, and before I knew it, Ryder and I were in stitches and wiping tears of laughter from our eyes.

"You can come to dinner too. There's no need to be dramatic," I said, patting Benny-cat's head. "You've been spending way too much time with Byrd."

As Ryder helped me up and we dusted off the remnants of snow from our clothes, the weight of the last few weeks evaporated. I looked up at the detective, the anticipation of our possible date humming in my chest.

This town may have had its problems, but that was why I loved it here more than anywhere else in the world. Only in Bluejay Falls could you get tackled by a hellhound disguised as a cat while being asked out on a date by a werewolf. It truly was a unique and exhilarating place to live.

ABOUT SEDONA JADE

Sedona Jade is the cozy side of a quirky coin; she channels her sarcasm not only into annoying her husband and children, but also into her characters as they stumble their way through unraveling mysteries. Embracing the charm of the cozy paranormal mystery genre, she spins tales set in small towns brimming with secret magic, peculiar happenings, and where a search in every nook and cranny could yield a clue. Her narratives intertwine the everyday with the supernatural, all laced with a generous helping of humor, sarcasm, and heart.

Away from the writing desk, she indulges in the simplicities of life—hiking, photography, and spending quality time with her family. At home, she's surrounded by a delightful mix of furry friends and an impressive assembly of reptiles, reflecting her love for all creatures great and small... including her belly-rub-loving sidekick, Faux the Arctic Fox!

www.sedonajade.com

ABOUT AMY STAKE

Amy Stake is a cozy mystery connoisseur and lover of all things paranormal. Much like a dragon, she loves collecting —aka hoarding—keyboards and all the pretty notebooks she can get her hands on. Amy is Sedona Jade's partner in paracozy crime… and with these two putting their wit and whimsical senses of humor together, you're guaranteed a wild ride of a story!